Miya's Mountain

Miya's Mountain

CATHY RINGLER

Crystal Publishing, LLC
Fort Collins, Colorado

To Ridge and River: two amazing cowkids.
May your lives be full of joy and adventure.

Chapter One

"But you promised!" Miya slumped against the old Ford truck. One hand clutched her useless phone. The other held a pair of rusted fencing pliers whose sharp edges dug into her palm.

Screech. The hinges on the horse trailer protested as Mom opened the back door to unload Dream, Miya's paint mare. She held out the lead rope, but Miya ignored it.

Her mom shrugged, tied up Dream, and jogged around the trailer to the tack compartment. She hauled out Miya's slicker and bridle. When Miya made no effort to help, Mom dumped the load on a flat rock.

"For the twentieth time…" Mother's patience had long since expired. "Blame the Forrest Service, not me. They're the ones who suddenly changed the lease dates." She held up an index finger. "Your dad is at the cattle sale." She held up a second finger. "I can't miss any more work." A third finger. "The fence has to be checked before we can turn out cows onto the leased land." A fourth finger. "We're out of time, and number five…" Mom's voice rose as she waved her thumb at Miya. "You're a part of this family, so step up and start taking responsibility. Why can't you think about anyone besides yourself?"

"That's not fair! I do take responsibility!" Miya protested. "You promised me! You promised I could go to the state track meet if Jake qualified. And you know how much that means to me. Why can't I be there to cheer him on? He always goes to my barrel races and supports me!"

Her mom sighed deeply. "Your boyfriend's a ranch kid. He'll understand."

Miya shook her head and stared at her phone. Not a single bar. Instead of glowering at her mother any longer, Miya let her imagination carry her away. Inside her head, a reel unfolded. She was at the track meet. She saw Jake sprint past the finish line. The girls' track team jumped up and down excitedly. Brinley and Aurora, the two fastest girls, showered him with hugs and high-fives. Jake basked in the attention of the gorgeous, skinny track team girls.

The truck door slammed, and the window slid down. "Dad will stop by with the empty trailer around six to pick you up."

"But, Mom, that's like ten hours from now."

"I know, so you better get riding." Mom hesitated for an instant and leaned out the window. "I'm sorry about the track meet, Miya. If I could, I'd take your place, but we have bills to pay." She cranked the ignition until the truck sputtered to life. "Lunch is in your saddle bag. Be careful. Love you."

Angry protests stuck in Miya's throat. The truck's window slid up, and her mom drove away—the trailer clattering over the washboards in the dirt road.

Miya watched the rig until the dust faded from view. She stomped toward Dream and shoved the fencing pliers into her saddle bag. Miya leaned into the paint, inhaling the good smells of horses, hay, and dust.

"I do take responsibility, Dream. I have a lot more chores than any other fifteen-year-old I know."

Zoey bounded across the pasture, carrying a stick. The border collie dropped it at Miya's feet. Eyes bright with anticipation, she watched Miya's every move.

"One time. That's it. Okay?" She picked up the stick and threw it as hard as she could. Zoey raced after it, returned within a few seconds, and dropped it on the ground. Miya knelt down and wrapped her arms around Zoey. "Sorry, girl. We'll play some more at lunch. We need to get going if we're going to ride around this whole pasture."

Miya held out her hand. "Shake?"

Zoey placed her paw in Miya's palm. "I promise we'll play later. Because, unlike *other* people, I always keep my promises."

Miya led Dream through the gate and stopped at the creek so her horse and dog could drink. Looking into the pool, she saw a wavy image of herself—a round-faced girl with dark eyes, a black braid threaded through the hole of a Cinch ballcap, and her usual hoodie and jeans under a stained Carhartt jacket.

"Boring clothes. Boring life."

Although she had never admitted it to anyone, occasionally Miya daydreamed that she had traded places with Aurora and Brinley. In this version of her life, she attended expensive sports camps. No more half-hearted crunches on a yoga mat in her room. Ever so casually, she laced up a new pair of Mizuno shoes before strolling out on the volleyball court, where all eyes and ears focused on her and her alone. Instead of counting on Jake for rides to school or taking the horrible bus home on the days he had practice, she drove a fancy truck. And rather than working herself to death all summer on the ranch, she snorkeled in the Caribbean and jet skied in Cancun.

Best of all, she'd be secure at the top of the food chain. Miya imagined herself sweeping through the halls at school, scrolling through her phone, chatting with a group of kids who stepped aside to include her.

"You think I need to get over missing the state track meet, don't you?" Miya sighed. Water dripped from Dream's whiskers as she raised her head and gazed at Miya. Her dream world vanished, plunging her once again into a reality she struggled to accept. "You might be right. I wish I had cell service, though, so I could text Jake and apologize again for not being there."

Mounting Dream, Miya followed the trail parallel to the fence. Although the calendar claimed it was May, winter had yet to surrender its frosty grip on the land. Piles of crusted snow nestled at the bases of the sagebrush. A chilly breeze swirled off the mountain and nipped the tips of Miya's ears. She zipped up her coat and hunched down into the saddle.

A meadowlark sang from a branch of a dead tree. Its yellow breast reminded Miya of the scarf Jake had given her last year. While riding along the fence line, Miya pictured Jake—the lock of dark hair that fell over his right eye when he told a story, the dimple that appeared and disappeared in his left cheek when he laughed, the twinkle in his eyes that lit up a room.

Miya rode a few more yards, where she noticed a snapped strand of barbed wire on the fence ahead. She pulled her gloves, the fencing pliers, and wire out of the saddlebags to repair the fence. Twenty-five minutes later, Miya stood back and surveyed her handiwork.

"That should hold. Come on, Zoey."

When they rounded a bend, Miya's stomach flipped. A mile section of fence lay on the ground—trampled posts and broken wires. "Wow! Some wolves or a bear must have chased a whole herd of elk through here. Even if I had enough posts and wire, I couldn't fix this mess alone. Dad's going to have to find time to help me."

Glancing at her watch, Miya saw it was only 11:00. Seven more hours until Dad got here… if she was lucky. Chances were that he'd spend another hour talking to his friends at the barn after the auction. They'd discuss the weather, the hay crop, and the darn fools in office. Meanwhile, she was stuck here. No phone, no friends, not even a fishing rod.

Chapter Two

By noon, Miya regretted storming away from the breakfast table, leaving behind two thick slices of her mom's signature banana bread. She was starving.

"Where should we stop to eat?" Miya asked Zoey. She glanced across the ridge tops and—*froze*. "Hey, Dream. Zoey. Look up there. A few hundred yards beyond those junipers. Do you see what I see?" Miya stood in her stirrups and concentrated. "That brown spot. It doesn't look like it belongs there. I think… I really think it's a huge elk antler!"

Miya's fingers tingled with excitement. Last year, after the elk and deer had shed their antlers, she and Jake found enough of them to pay for a new bull riding rope for Jake and two pairs of cute new jeans for her. They'd laughed about how rich people from other states over-decorated their houses with elk horn lamps, chandeliers, chairs, and mirrors for a Western look. Those same people clomped around town in new boots and designer jeans, oblivious that their cowboy hats were on backward. Miya giggled, remembering the sea of backward cowboy hats at the Fourth of July rodeo.

It was time to stop daydreaming and start making money. Miya tapped Dream with her heels. "Come on. Let's go check it out!"

At the bottom of the ridge, Miya studied the red rock rising abruptly from the foothills. Brown ribbons of elk trails crisscrossed the muddy sides. "It's steep, Dream, but I really want that antler.

It's got to weigh ten pounds, and at eighteen dollars a pound… and maybe we'll be lucky and find its mate, too, so if we double that—"

Miya stared at the antler. "You know what I think, girl? If the elk climbed that ridge, so can we."

Miya pointed Dream toward a trail that wound around a sidehill into the timber. The mare climbed cautiously, pushing through the pebbly snow drifts that occasionally obscured the path. Before they entered the woods, Miya glanced back at the fence. By now, it was so small that it reminded her of a toy in a kid's farm set. When they reached the timberline, a cloud obscured the sun. The wind picked up. *Creak. Creak.* The trees swayed to and fro as she and Dream wove in and out of the shadows.

The mare was breathing heavily now. Miya leaned forward to encourage her. "It's not much farther, I promise."

Just then, Dream stumbled and fell onto her knees. Her hooves churned as she struggled to regain her balance. As Miya was thrown forward in the saddle, she realized that under the thin layer of mud lay a sheet of solid ice.

With a massive heave, Dream regained her footing. Miya jumped off. Since there was no place level enough to stop, Miya stumbled up the hill alongside the paint.

There it was. The antler. Only six feet away. So close that Miya could see its eight sharp points. She could almost feel the solid weight of the beams. Still leading Dream, Miya grabbed onto a bush and hauled herself up the hill. The muscles in her calves strained as her boots slipped backward.

"Come on." Miya gasped. "Almost there." As Miya reached out to grasp one of the white tipped tines, she slipped, falling to her knees. In a millisecond, the rocks shifted underfoot and began rolling down the side of the hill. They showered the ridge with bumps and pings. Zoey yelped, but Miya was too busy scrambling for a handhold to help her.

Miya fell flat on her belly, smacking her chin and scraping her face along the rough terrain. Faster and faster, she slid down the steep side of the ridge. Miya knew the edge of the cliff was close. She pictured its jutting layers high above the tops of the trees. Miya dug her fingers into the earth, clawing at the icy mud.

I don't want to die here!

Miya's boot hit something solid. She looked down to see it wedged against the root of a juniper. The bush was just a scrub, twisted and barely hanging onto life at the edge of the canyon. Beyond it, the world dropped away.

Heart pounding, Miya surveyed the situation. She hadn't fallen far, only fifteen feet or so. She looked over the side of the canyon. Jagged rocks rose knifelike above the treetops. Miya imagined herself falling into nothingness. Thudding against boulders. Ending in a crumpled heap by the river. Would the ravens peck out her eyes like they did with a baby calf? Would the bears and wolves fight over her flesh? Dizziness rolled over Miya in waves. Black spots clouded her vision. Sweat gathered under her armpits.

A shower of sand and pebbles forced Miya to open her eyes. Zoey raced over and licked her ear, nose, and mouth. Tears streamed down Miya's cheeks, and Zoey licked those, too.

Miya saw Dream standing sideways on the elk trail, her reins dangling. "I *have* to make it up to Dream. I *have* to get her down safely." She had heard stories about horses who'd rolled off the side of the mountain, either killing them or injuring them so badly that they had to be put down.

Flexing her fingers, Mia reached for a rock with her left hand. She tested it. Solid. Miya dug the fingers of her right hand into the dirt. With her heart banging against her ribs, Miya counted, "One, two, three, go!" Straining her arms and digging her toes into the ground, Miya kicked and clawed. Centimeter by centimeter, she squirmed over cactuses and sharp stones.

Miya rested when she reached a small rocky shelf. Trembling, she gathered herself for one last effort—she rose to her hands and knees and started crawling uphill. From above, Dream nickered.

"I'm coming, Dream. Hang on, girl."

Miya collapsed in front of Dream. Closing her eyes to pull herself together, she drew in shuddering gasps of air. Dream nickered again and blew softly on the back of Miya's neck. "Sorry, I got you into this, Dream." Facedown in the dirt, Miya's words were muffled.

Grabbing her stirrup, Miya pulled herself to her feet. Rocks, some as small as pebbles, others as large as her fist, shifted under her boots. After finding her balance, Miya gathered her courage and looked down. It was as though she were perched on the roof of a tall building. The deer below were small dark spots on the valley floor. Miya swayed. Bile rose in her throat.

"Dream, I know it's scary, but you need to turn downhill, head-first, so your back feet won't fall off the trail and start sliding like mine did. I'll scoot on my butt for the steepest part, then crawl to that big rock. After that, maybe I can stand." Miya wiped her palm on her thighs. She wrapped the reins around her hand. "I'll keep ahold of you. If one of us starts sliding, maybe the other can stop them."

Deep in her heart, Miya knew she couldn't save a thousand-pound horse if it started to fall, but this was Dream, and losing her was unthinkable.

Sitting down, Miya bent her knees, bringing them up close to her chest. She dug in the heels of her boots and curled her fingers into the icy ground. After whistling for Zoey, Miya started her descent—slipping and sliding down the mountain.

Half an hour later, Miya stumbled to the fence on shaky legs. Her nails were broken and bleeding. Her calves were sore from cramping.

Breathing hard, Miya cupped Dream's muzzle in her hand. She leaned down and kissed the mare's velvety nose. Miya scratched

Zoey behind her ears, wishing she could ride back to the gate, curl up beside her dog in the soft grass by the creek, and sleep until Dad picked her up. That was impossible, of course. She had already wasted over two hours, but Dad needed to know about the condition of the fence. Miya brushed herself off and, with herculean effort, mounted Dream.

Chapter Three

"What do you mean you didn't make it all the way around?" Dad's hands tightened on the steering wheel. "How am I supposed to know how many posts and how much wire to buy?"

Miya swallowed. The Snickers bar her dad had bought her lay unopened in her lap.

"Dad, I wanted to find it and its mate and—"

Her dad interrupted her thoughts. "What does that have to do with the fence?"

Miya hesitated. "Well, uh, Dream and I tried to climb up to get the antler, but the ground was way too slippery."

"Of course, it was. That ice on the north side of the ridge won't melt for another month at least."

Miya wished she had thought of that before she started up the hill. She rubbed her finger across the candy bar wrapper before continuing the story. "I slipped and fell. I was pretty close to the side of the cliff, so I had to crawl some of the way out."

Dad glared at her, then back at the road. The silence stretched as far as the empty highway in front of them.

"That whole thing took so much time that I couldn't ride all the way around the pasture."

Still, Dad didn't speak. His eyebrows drew into a frown.

Finally, Miya whispered, "Sorry about the fence, Dad."

Dad hit the steering wheel with his palm. "To hell with the fence! You could have died out there. You could have killed Dream!"

"I know, Dad." Miya bit her lip. "That's all I can think about. That and letting you down."

"Last week, you left the gate open, so the heifers got out. Yesterday, you forgot to turn off the horses' water and flooded the corrals, and today, you took your horse up the side of the mountain on some wild goose chase. You're *fifteen*! I should be able to trust you to finish a simple job!"

Dad grabbed a cup from the holder and tilted his head back, draining the last sip of coffee. He crumpled the cup and tossed it into the back seat. He hunched over the steering wheel and stared at the road.

Miya looked out her window, fighting back shame and tears. Finally, she asked, "Did the sale go okay?"

Her dad shook his head. "Not really."

"I'll wake up early tomorrow and finish riding the fence. You'll still have time to drive to town and buy the stuff to fix it. We'll build it the next day."

"We'll see." The flat tone in his voice said it all—he didn't trust her anymore.

Miya stared into the empty darkness. After a few more miles, she slipped the Snickers bar into the door pocket underneath a crumpled fast-food bag.

The next morning, Miya found a note and the Snickers bar from the truck on the kitchen table. The note read: CARTER IS HELPING ME FIX FENCE. SORRY, I WAS SO HARD ON YOU LAST NIGHT. DAD.

Miya reread the note, unsure of how she felt about it. At first, she was relieved because she hated building fence. It was hot and boring. However, the relief was short-lived. Miya knew Carter, their hired man, already had a long list of more important things to do.

Guilt gnawed at Miya's conscience. *You were the one who messed up. You should be the one to fix it.*

Miya shrugged and argued with the voice in her head. *I can't change anything now. It's not like I can hike to the trailhead, but I can eat this piece of toast and ride Mesa. I'll help Dad with another chore later.*

Mesa was an adopted Mustang—iron gray with three dark stockings and a thick black mane. Six months ago, Mesa wouldn't let Miya touch him. He'd pin his ears back, stomp, and snort. He had even kicked her once, leaving a hoofprint-shaped bruise on her upper thigh. But the young horse was coming around thanks to Jake's help and her patience.

Inside the barn door, Miya waited for her eyes to adjust to the dimness. Dust moats floated in a shaft of sunlight. Cheeping sparrows played tag in the rafters.

Miya saddled Mesa and led him outside. She gazed northward, where puffy clouds gathered, pooling in the canyons and drifting along the ridges. The grass behind her rustled. *Shh, Shh, Shh, Shh.* Miya spun around, poised to face a rattlesnake.

Instead, a cottontail hopped out of the tall grass. The rabbit froze—its liquid-brown eyes fixated on Miya before ducking under the horse trailer.

"Just a rabbit. Guess I'm still a little jumpy after almost falling off the mountain yesterday."

Miya tightened the cinch, swung into the saddle, and whistled for Zoey. She signaled Mesa to move off down the lane. As she rode, Miya thought about Jake. His team won the relay yesterday only because Jake had made up a lot of lost time as the anchor. He was everybody's hero. Again.

Brinley had posted a picture of him breaking the finish line tape. The caption read: JAKE IS ON FIRE. There were over one hundred likes and more than forty comments. Most of them from girls. Grinding her teeth, Miya read each one.

She knew Jake never bothered to read comments, but even if he did read some of these, he'd simply shrug them off with a laugh. Not Miya! The words, trapped in her head, swirled round and round. She sighed. Thankfully, it was almost summer, so she wouldn't have to deal with the popular girls for a few months.

An hour later, Miya dismounted and rubbed Mesa's neck. "You're doing much better. You only shied at four big rocks, two downed trees, and one sage hen."

She leaned closer and pretended to whisper in Mesa's ear. "I don't blame you for being scared of the plastic bag caught in the fence. When the wind blew that thing loose, I jumped, too."

"Let's ride to the top of this hill, switchback down to the creek, and head home." When Mesa took his first steps, Miya's stomach felt weird, like an entire greasy pizza was roiling in the bottom of it. Her heart pounded. Her skin was clammy.

"Why am I so nervous?" Miya asked Mesa. "This is the easy way up the hill. If you collapse in the middle of it, you won't slide backward any more than ten inches."

Still, Miya's heart pounded harder—beating all the way down to the soles of her boots. She slid off Mesa. "No worries. I'll lead you to the top." She wiped the sweat from her forehead, breathed deeply, and took a step. One. Two. Three more steps.

She stopped and studied the rim of the hill up above. The thought of looking over the top made her body feel tense and heavy. She tried to take another step, but her legs were dead weight.

"I must be getting sick. I better not go up there feeling like this. Mesa, you're only a colt, and you've already shied a bunch today. If I fall off, I could break a leg or something."

Yet, in the pit of her stomach, where the imaginary pizza still churned, Miya was overcome by an immense sense of shame. How could she be so afraid of such a little hill?

Chapter Four

Three weeks later, Miya clung tightly to the railing, summoning the courage to walk down the stairs—stairs she had climbed up and down daily without a thought. She heard Dad's voice from his office.

"I'm sorry. My client's fishing trip has been booked for over a year. No amount of money is going to change that." Miya glanced into the room. Dad was on the phone again, staring at the desk calendar in front of him. "I understand that your son is only here for a long weekend." He ran a hand through his hair and frowned.

Miya crept downstairs and crossed the hall into the kitchen, where her mother sat at the table, chewing on a pencil. Miya hesitated a few seconds, taking in her mom's slumped shoulders, her pained expression, and the strands of gray threading her hair.

Mom's hand was pressed against her forehead as she stared at the budget notebook in front of her. When she saw Miya, she snapped the notebook shut and turned it over—but not before Miya had caught a glimpse of numbers crossed out and circled in red.

Although her stomach flip-flopped, Miya pretended she hadn't seen the red numbers marching across the pages. "Who's Dad talking to?"

Mom rubbed the back of her neck. "Someone who wants to book a fishing trip to Wildcat Falls. Could you get me an aspirin, please?"

Miya plunked a bottle of generic aspirin on the table along with a glass of water. Dad was still talking. She opened the refrigerator and feigned interest in the contents just so she could eavesdrop a little longer.

His voice drifted into the kitchen from beyond the open office door. "I know we have great reviews. And yes, Skippingbird Outfitters is a newer business with a reputation to build, but I still can't help you."

Miya closed the refrigerator door and peeked into the office. Dad was pinching the bridge of his nose.

"No, I can't cancel my trip for double the money." A pause. "Not even triple." Another pause. Dad's voice rose in disbelief. "Five times?"

Miya's mother pushed her chair back and headed into the office. She stood beside her husband, studying the desk calendar.

Miya watched as her dad attempted to speak but was interrupted. He broke a pencil in two. One half skittered across the desk and onto the floor.

Grabbing the budget notebook and tearing out a sheet of paper, Miya looked around the kitchen for something to write with. She saw the dry-erase marker hanging by the scheduling board. Miya uncapped the marker and wrote in large black letters: I CAN TAKE THE TRIP. She ran into the office and stopped in front of Dad. Miya pointed to the paper and held it up. He read it, frowned, and shook his head. Nodding her head hard, up and down, Miya jabbed each word with her finger. "Please," she mouthed.

Dad raised his eyebrows, shook his head again, and turned his back. "As I was saying, if anything happens to change, I'll let you know."

He hung up the phone. Without looking at Miya, Dad lifted his straw cowboy hat off the rack. "Got to go. I'm late for a meeting with the Forest Service." He kissed Miya's mom on the cheek.

"Don't hold supper for me. I need to swing by the feed store while I'm in town."

Miya clutched his arm. "Wait, Dad. The guy's offering a lot of money. Why can't I take the trip?"

He exhaled. "Because you're fifteen. And... remember what happened not too long ago when you were supposed to be riding fence?"

"I know, but that won't happen again. I promise. I've been up to Wildcat Falls a hundred times. I'm ready to take a pack trip on my own."

"Think about it. I'll have the horses and pack equipment with me. We can only book one trip at a time."

Miya opened her mouth to argue, but Dad held up his hand. "End of discussion. I really have to go."

The screen door slammed behind him. Miya wadded up the paper and threw it toward the trashcan. It teetered on the rim and fell to the floor.

In an outburst of anger and frustration, Miya stormed over to her mom and fumed, "I am *not* too young! And five times the usual cost is a whole lot of money!"

"I agree with you about the money part, but you can't change the fact that those dates are already booked."

"Even if they weren't, he'd never let me go. Dad doesn't trust me."

Miya's mom hugged her, but Miya stood as stiff as a fence post. Her jaw ached from clenching it so tightly.

"It's not that he doesn't trust you. A client puts their life in your hands up there. It's a huge responsibility."

Miya sighed. "I understand that. Plus, I know I made a mistake by trying to reach the elk horn, but I learned something. Why can't Dad let that be the end of the story?"

She strode angrily to the window and gripped the sill to calm herself down. After taking a deep breath, Miya spoke to her mom's reflection. "If it were up to you and we had extra horses and gear, would *you* let me take the trip?"

Picking up the crumpled paper, Mom threw it into the trashcan. "I'd give it some serious thought. Like you said, five times is a whole lot of money."

Mom was on her side, so that was something. Even if she could change Dad's mind, she still needed horses and equipment. The only horses left at the ranch would be Dream and Dollar, the naughty pony too small for grownups to ride.

Miya's eyes fell on a framed picture. It was taken at the fair when she and Jake were about three. They were both riding the merry-go-round. Jake rode a black stallion, and Miya perched on a silver unicorn. Miya picked up the picture from the office desk and smiled. Even back then, she and Jake had been best friends.

And suddenly, Miya had the solution. Jake! She could ask Jake for help. His family had horses and pack equipment. Why not rent the necessary equipment from them? Her dad might be open to that idea…if only he could forget about last month.

Miya hooked a boot heel over the rung of her chair and glanced around the Runningdeers' kitchen. A cast iron griddle spanned two burners on the stovetop. The smell of pancakes and bacon hung in the air.

Jake sat beside Miya—his arm thrown loosely around the back of her chair. He'd been irrigating earlier and now had a spot of mud on his cheek. Miya itched to reach over and brush it off, but instead, she turned back to Jake's mom, Janelle, and continued her explanation.

"Dad has a trip already booked, but if we could rent some of your horses, pack equipment, and horse trailer, we could still make good money, and so could you."

Janelle reached over and laid a hand on top of Miya's. Her eyes were warm and brown, the color of hot fudge. "Even if we did that, honey, it's not going to change the fact that your dad thinks you're too young to take the trip."

"Five times the money. Dad won't admit it, but that would be such a big help." And, Miya thought, there might be enough money left over for some cute new clothes—some fun things to wear to school like Converse high tops. Not the platform ones.

"I'd go with you," Jake said, interrupting her thoughts, "but I don't think that would solve the problem with your dad."

Drover, Jake's new puppy, appeared at the screen door. He scratched at it and whined. His furry body wriggled enthusiastically when he spotted the three of them at the table. Jake opened the door, scooped up the pup, and plunked him into Miya's lap.

Giggling, she tried to fend off Drover's slobbery advances. "You'd go to the mountains with me, wouldn't you, boy?"

Janelle leaned forward in her chair. "This is really important to you, isn't it?"

Miya nodded. "When will Dad understand that he needs to stop punishing me for what I did a few weeks ago? I told him I was sorry, and it wouldn't happen again. Why can't he trust me now?"

"I don't think he means to punish you," Janelle said. "We were all scared when we found out what happened. Your dad most of all."

"Grr!" There were no words to express her frustration. Miya wished she'd never spotted that stupid antler.

"You know, trust needs to be earned," Janelle said.

"I just need another chance to earn it!" Miya swallowed hard. "I'd better go." She set Drover down on the floor and bent down to give him one last pat.

"What would you think if Jake and I both rode along on the trip?" Janelle asked.

Miya looked up. "You'd do that?"

Janelle picked up a rubber hot dog and squeaked it twice. She tossed it to Drover, who happily pounced on it. "Wildcat Falls is close to our lease, and I need to check the cows up there anyway. I'm sure I can manage a few days off work. What do you say, Jake?"

"A couple of days fishing in the mountains?" Jake grinned at Miya. "I think I could be persuaded."

Miya hugged Janelle and blew Jake a kiss. "Janelle Runningdeer, you and your son are the best! Now, all I need to do is convince my dad!" She leaned down and scratched Drover behind the ears. "Bye, cutie. I better go home and do my chores before Jake rides tonight."

Still smiling, Miya stood up to leave. "See you at the rodeo."

Chapter Five

Miya unsnapped her seatbelt. "Bye, Dad. Remember, Jake's bringing me home tonight." Her dad's phone rang. He glanced at it and muttered, "That guy again." He pressed decline.

"Was that the same person who called this afternoon?"

"Yep." He pointed to a familiar red pickup. "There's the Runningdeers' rig. I told Michael I'd meet him by the gate. Tell Jake to make us proud." Dad stepped out and slammed the door.

Miya dabbed on some strawberry lip gloss and slid out of the truck. Her footsteps crunched on the gravel. She started toward the side of the arena where the rough stock, the bucking horses, and bulls burst out of the chutes and performed for the crowd. Zipping up her jacket, Miya watched the cowboys bring the saddle broncs up the alley. Puffing up dust, they trotted with long strides— manes and tails streaming. Miya's fingers itched for her colored pencils to sketch the collage of bays, blacks, and paints. Instead, she took out her phone and snapped a picture. Maybe she'd draw the horses tomorrow.

Miya found Jake behind the chutes. Tonight, he wore a bright green cowboy shirt the same color as the fringe on his chaps. Jake's right sleeve was rolled up. He wrapped athletic tape slowly and precisely around his wrist. From the way Jake stared at the tape, Miya knew he was deep inside his head, visualizing his ride.

"Hey, Jake." Miya stepped in front of him.

Jake looked up and grinned down—the dimple appeared on his left cheek. Miya wanted to touch it, but other bull riders were watching. Instead, she stuffed her hands into her back pockets and smiled back.

Miya cleared her throat. "Dad's expecting you to make us proud tonight."

Jake tore the tape off with his teeth and flexed his wrist. "I'll do my best." He smiled at her again. Jake picked up his protective vest and checked the pocket for his mouthguard. "Can you video? Mom's not here tonight. Last couple of times, I messed up right out of the chute, so I need the first jump."

Miya's heart fluttered. She put her hand on her chest and rubbed it. Video Jake? To film the bull's first jump out, she'd have to climb to the very top of the bleachers. Since the cliff incident, everything seemed so high and frightening. Yesterday, she could barely force herself to stand on a chair to reach the shelf in her closet. Miya's shoulders drooped as she stared at a crushed pop can wedged under a stack of metal posts. She knew how the can felt.

"I, um…I'm not sure," she stuttered.

Jake, looking over the fence at the pen of bulls, didn't seem to hear. He slid his coiled bull rope over his shoulder. The bell buckled to the bottom of the rope clanged. Jake gave her a quick hug and started toward the catwalk. "Thanks, Miya," Jake called over his shoulder. "Wish me luck."

Miya swallowed and whispered back, "Wish me luck, too."

She watched Jake join the group of other bull riders. She heard a short burst of laughter followed by the rise and fall of voices. For the hundredth time in her life, Miya wished she had Jake's confidence.

Miya turned away and flipped her braid over her shoulder. Trudging across the dusty gravel, Miya headed toward the bleachers. Tinny-sounding music streamed from the speakers. Her stomach churned. She needed to use the restroom but didn't have time to hike the quarter mile to the rodeo office and back to the contestant stands before the bull riding. She refused to use one of the closer smelly outhouses. *No, thank you.* Trusting that her stomach would calm down, she waited. Miya turned her face upward toward the breeze. It carried the smell of cows and popcorn and greasy French fries. The queasy feeling returned.

By the time Miya reached the stands and glanced into the arena, the clown and his mini donkey were in the middle of it. The donkey grabbed the clown's red bandanna. He shook it side to side while the clown in clumsy yellow shoes chased him. The crowd erupted in laughter. The familiar cadence of the announcer's voice and the clown's antics soothed Miya. Like everyone who competed regularly in this rodeo, she knew all the jokes by heart.

Miya grabbed the metal railing of the contestant stands. It was cold and slick beneath her hand. She had to hurry. During the clown act, cowboys loaded the bulls into the chutes. The riders were prepared to climb on the bull as soon as the chute boss signaled.

Miya let go of the railing, wiped her palms on the thighs of her jeans, and grabbed it again. After taking a deep breath, she put her foot on the first step.

"One down," she whispered to herself. "Nine to go." Miya held more tightly to the railing. Her knuckles turned white. She ordered herself to pick up her boot and place it on the next step. "Two down. Up on the third." Miya paused, waiting for her heart to slow down.

She could make it to the top. Only six more steps to go. Then she'd tackle the bleachers. Or maybe not. Maybe she could see well enough from the bottom to get the shot Jake wanted. Miya climbed onto the fourth step. She chewed the lip gloss off her bottom lip.

Five steps. Six steps. Seven steps. Miya realized she was holding her breath, so she stopped and forced herself to breathe. Every time she climbed a stair, the railing creaked. Miya pictured the rusted bolts snapping and the entire staircase collapsing into a skeleton of twisted metal. Just like on the mountain, she'd have no control. Only this time, she'd be hurled onto concrete instead of jagged rocks.

"Excuse me," came a demanding voice from behind her.

Miya jumped. Still holding tightly to the rail as though her life depended on it, she turned and saw a woman snapping pink gum and holding a cellphone to her ear.

"You're blocking the way," the woman said. "I need to get up there to watch the bull riding."

Miya pressed herself against the rail. "Oh, sorry."

The gum lady brushed by, followed by a boy of about ten. Although it was still warm outside, his black Under Armor jacket was zipped nearly to the top. As the boy drew even with her, Miya wrinkled her nose at a musky smell.

"Wanna see?" Using his right hand, the boy unzipped his jacket a few inches and reached into his pocket. He opened his palms to reveal two tiny balls of fur. The animals were a little smaller than gerbils. They had bulging eyes and fluffy tails. Their cream-colored foreheads were decorated with a triangle of brown fur.

Miya let go of the railing and stuck out a finger to touch one of the tiny creatures. "Are those—?"

"Sugar gliders," the boy finished for her. "Shh," he gestured toward his mother with his chin. "She doesn't know I brought them along."

"They're super cute. What are their names?"

"Jellybean and Bubble Gum."

Before Miya could reply, she caught a fleeting glimpse of straw cowboy hats, dirty faces, and Yellowstone National Park T-shirts. She watched as three kids barreled down the steps toward them. Miya reached back and gripped the railing for dear life.

A freckle-faced girl was last in line. Most of her wispy red hair had escaped her ponytail and fallen into her eyes. She pushed it back with one hand while dragging a torn blue blanket with the other.

"Wait for me, or I'm telling!"

When the girl looked up, her feet caught in the blanket, and she pitched forward, falling into the boy with the black jacket, who stumbled into Miya. Quicker than a horsefly bites, one of the sugar gliders jumped out of the boy's hand and onto the bleachers.

"Eek!" The little girl's shriek drowned out the announcer. "It's a rat!"

"It's not a rat. It's a sugar glider!" the boy screamed. He grabbed for Jellybean, but the sugar glider was too quick.

Open-mouthed, Miya watched as Jellybean ran up the stairs and started along the first set of bleachers. Jellybean ran across a woman's sandaled foot. Seeming to ignore the screams, he skipped up to the next row, sending a box of popcorn flying. The sugar glider stopped for an instant, sniffing the white kernels scattered beside him.

"Grab him!" the boy yelled as he scrambled up the steps. But before anyone could react, Jellybean was gone.

The sugar glider brushed by a paper cup, spilling ice and brown pop onto the seat and spattering the bleachers below. A teenage girl scooted sideways. "Hey! This is my new shirt!"

"I can't believe you brought those things!" The gum lady stormed toward them from the other side of the bleachers. Reaching the boy, she stomped her foot so hard that the aluminum floor vibrated. Jellybean turned and ran back along the way he'd come. Miya tilted her head and strained to see around the crowd.

Reversing directions, Jellybean shimmied up one of the poles that supported the canopy on the bleachers. When he reached the top, he spread his wings and glided all the way down, landing at Miya's feet.

"Grab him before he runs to the parking lot!"

Both Miya and Jellybean froze. She tried to pry her fingers open, but they seemed molded to the railing.

"Grab him! He'll get run over!"

Miya's fingers tingled. She glanced at the ground, at the cracks in the concrete below.

Jellybean gazed up at her, wiggling his pink nose. "I can do this," Miya whispered. "I have to do this." She fell to her knees and cupped her hands over him. His soft fur brushed her palms. Breathing hard, Miya waited as the boy ran over, stooped down, and gathered up the sugar glider.

"Thanks," the boy said, settling Jellybean into his pocket. He looked over his shoulder. "Meet you at the car, Mom."

"Wait," Miya said. She climbed unsteadily to her feet. "Can that thing really fly?"

The boy glanced toward his mom again. "He can't fly, only glides, like a flying squirrel. Gotta go." The boy jumped off the stairs and disappeared.

"You're grounded for the rest of your life!" The woman stepped on Miya's boot as she stormed past, still snapping her gum.

Just then, the announcer interrupted the chaos. "Jake Runningdeer is making a heck of a ride."

Miya groaned. She didn't have time to get her phone out of her pocket, much less find a place where she could see. The buzzer sounded. Jake's score was announced. The crowd cheered. Miya dropped her head to her chest and squeezed her eyes shut.

Inching around and without looking over the side, Miya concentrated on putting her foot down one step, then another, and another until she finally reached solid ground. Miya exhaled in a thankful sigh. It had been even more terrifying going down the stairs than climbing up.

Miya stepped under the bleachers and leaned against one of the support poles. She glanced around in the fading light. The ground was littered with nacho boxes and crumpled paper cups. A small gray bird pecked daintily at a chunk of hamburger bun.

She crouched down and put her head in her hands. "I let Jake down again," she whispered. Miya breathed in and out, forehead resting in her cupped palms. *What is wrong with me? Why can't I stop these worries? What if I have to live with them forever?* Miya clenched and unclenched her fists. Maybe it was time to face up to what had happened. Maybe that was the first step in getting back to normal.

Her phone buzzed with a text from Jake.

    Where are u?

Sighing, Miya stepped over a puddle of melted snow cones and set out to find him.

As she crossed the parking lot, Miya heard high-pitched squeals of laughter. She poked her head around a horse trailer and saw Aurora and Brinley sitting on the tailgate of Jake's truck. Jake stood a couple of feet away, his head thrown back, laughing with the girls.

Miya frowned. *Those two never come to the rodeo unless they have a specific reason. Like Jake.* She glared at them, wondering if they'd looked up "edgy western clothing" on their mother's Pinterest account. Real competitors didn't wear shorts with cowboy boots or a fringed vest over a skimpy crop top.

Brinley pushed away from the side of the truck and stepped closer to Jake, reaching out to touch his arm. She was thin and nearly as tall as Jake. Her shoulder-length hair created a perfect blond curtain that shimmered in the parking lot lights.

Miya snorted. *What's up with Brinley?* She knew Jake was taken.

"I'm going to text Miya again." Jake took a step back.

"Don't bother." Miya forced herself to emerge from behind the trailer. "I'm here."

Jake's face broke into a grin. "Miya, where've you been?"

"Over by the contestant stands." Miya refused to admit she had been hiding behind a horse trailer all along so she wouldn't have to deal with Aurora and Brinley.

Miya watched the girls inspect her. She tried to suck in her stomach, but there was no way to hide its roundness, her flyaway hair, or the shiny concealer on her pimple. Miya knew they wondered why in the world Jake stayed with her when he could do so much better.

"Jake," Aurora said, turning away and ignoring Miya, "I already posted about your ride, but I'll send you the whole video."

Jake tossed his rigging bag into the bed of the truck. "You don't have to. Miya got it."

Miya's cheeks burned. Hot tears pricked behind her eyelids. She cleared her throat. "Actually. I didn't."

Jake looked at her, surprised. "You didn't?" He shrugged. "That's okay. Sure, send it, Aurora."

Aurora, shorter than Brinley but just as blond and thin, raised her eyebrows and smirked. The heat from Miya's cheeks spread to the tips of her ears. The nagging voice inside her head sneered. *While Aurora was busy videoing Jake's entire ride, you couldn't even make it to the top of the stairs.*

"Ready, Miya?" Jake waved to the girls. "See you guys later."

Brinley stepped backward, blocking the driver's door. "Don't forget the track picnic tomorrow night. And the party afterward."

Jake took Miya's hand. "Thanks for reminding me, but I'm hanging out with Miya."

"Oh…" Brinley looked down her nose at Miya. "It's just for team members, but I suppose *she* could come."

Jake squeezed Miya's hand. "No thanks, Brinley. Miya and I have other plans."

"I can't believe those two." Miya tossed her ball cap on the dash. "Brinley is so into you that it's pathetic. Why is she even after you? I thought she had a boyfriend."

Jake laughed and reached for her hand. "She's not into me. We're just friends from track."

"Just friends? Really?"

Shrugging, Jake said, "Yep, that's all on my part."

She stared out the window. *Guys are so oblivious sometimes.* She watched the horse trailers pull out of the parking lot and thought of every good comeback she should have made to Brinley.

"Why didn't you get the video? Did you run into somebody and not make it to the stands in time?"

Miya turned from the window. She chewed on a fingernail. *Should I tell him the real reason? Admit that I can't walk up a flight of stairs without feeling like I'm going to faint? Maybe I should start with the easy stuff.* So, she described the boy, the sugar gliders, the girl with the blue blanket, and the gum lady with the cellphone.

At the end of the story, Jake laughed and shook his head. "I can understand why you were a little distracted."

Miya rubbed her finger along the calluses on his hand. She took a deep breath. "There's another reason. I should have been on the top bleacher before the whole thing started tonight. Sorry, I didn't get your video."

"Like I told you the last twelve times you apologized, Miya, it's fine. You can stop apologizing now. I just wish I could have seen those sugar gliders."

Sighing, Miya laid her head on Jake's shoulder. The cab of his truck smelled familiar and comforting—dogs, horses, liniment, Taco Bell.

"Don't worry. You'll get it next time."

"Only what if I can't?" The words dropped like stones into the darkness between them.

"What did you say?"

Miya's cheeks burned with shame. How could she tell him about these crazy fears? The ones that prodded her awake in the morning. Miya hid her face in Jake's shirt, the fabric scratchy against her face.

"Tell me." He tugged gently on her braid.

Miya sat up and swallowed. "Something's been happening to me lately. I worry all the time and keep looking over my shoulder, expecting something terrible to happen." Miya closed her eyes. "For a while now, when I try to climb something, I freeze. Finally, I googled it. I guess I'm having some kind of anxiety. Almost panic attacks."

"Attacks? Have you had more than one?"

Miya opened her eyes. She focused on wadding up the hem of her jacket and then smoothing it out. "I haven't been able to go up into the hayloft all week, and remember last Friday when you wanted me to bring a hammer when you were fixing the shed roof?"

Jake nodded.

"I pretended I didn't hear you calling because I was afraid to go up the ladder. I couldn't force myself to climb the steps to the bleachers tonight. I tried and tried, but my feet wouldn't work right." Miya wiped her eyes with her palms. "Poor Jellybean almost got run over because I couldn't let go of the railing to grab him."

Jake pulled her back against him. "But you found a way, and you saved him." He brushed his cheek against her hair. "This height thing. I don't understand it. When you were little, you were always climbing trees. Remember when your mom had to call the fire department because you climbed so high up in that cottonwood tree by the road?"

"I know. I'd give anything to feel normal again."

Jake hugged her. "When have you ever been normal?" he teased. "Who have you told so far?"

Miya held up three fingers. "Dream, Zoey, and you."

The parking lot was nearly empty. Jake started the truck and shifted it into gear. "Your horse, your dog, and me." He pulled out onto the main road. "I'm honored to be included in such good company."

"You should be." Miya laughed. "It's a very select group."

"Do your mom and dad know?

"Of course not. If they did, they wouldn't consider letting me take the trip. Besides, they're both so busy trying to keep the place afloat that they haven't noticed anything different about me."

Jake turned onto Miya's road. He drove in silence until he reached her house. Pulling up to the porch, he asked, "How will the fishing trip work? If you can't make it up the bleachers, what's going to happen when you try to ride over the pass into camp?"

Miya rubbed her temples, where a headache was gaining momentum. "The trip is a couple of weeks away. I've been watching YouTube videos. If I do breathing exercises and some other YouTube stuff, I'm sure I can fix it. At least well enough to ride over the pass.

"From what you told me, I think you need more help than random videos."

Miya stiffened. She wished this whole terrible night would end. First, the bleacher incident; then, Brinley's flirting; and now, Jake questioning her ability. It was one thing for her dad to think she wasn't capable, but it was something else for Jake to come right out and say it.

"That's mean." Miya clenched her jaw and gritted her teeth. The headache was about to take on a life of its own.

Jake held up both hands. "I'm not trying to be mean. I'm being honest. Why don't you tell your mom tomorrow? She'll probably have some good ideas."

Miya picked up her ball cap and shoved it onto her head. She stormed out of the truck and slammed the door.

Jake rolled down the window. "Hey, don't be mad. I only said something because I care about you. You should take my advice."

"I'll think about it." Miya stamped toward the porch.

Chapter Six

Sunlight poured through the slatted shades of Miya's window and cast kaleidoscopic patterns on her teal rug. Miya stared at the bright lines between the dark shadows. She turned her head to look at the clock. 9:42. *9:42!* Her parents never let her sleep that late. She had chores to do.

Miya rolled out of bed and twisted her hair into a messy bun. She opened the bottom dresser drawer—not one pair of clean jeans. She'd have to do laundry. Meanwhile, Miya scooped up some pants from the floor and gave them a hard shake. Last year, a scorpion had hidden in a pair she'd left on the floor. After the scorpion stung her, the welt throbbed like a bee sting.

She shook the jeans out one more time—just to be safe—and pulled them on. To her surprise, they hung loosely on her hips. Stretched out? Or had she lost a little weight these past few months? Oh well, she'd never be as skinny as the track team girls.

After pulling a T-shirt over her head, Miya picked up her boots and ran a finger over the ragged hole on the side of the right one. The leather had torn through the stitches and pulled away from the sole. Miya had glued it together once upon a time, but the glue didn't hold. She'd thought about wrapping duct tape around the boot, but her parents would notice a big silver glob on the side of her foot. No way Miya was going to let them write *New boots for Miya* in the budget notebook.

Miya turned the boot over and shook the sand out. If her dad let her take the trip, she could buy herself a new pair of cowboy boots. In fact, she could buy new boots for all of them.

After coaching herself down the stairs, Miya stopped at the kitchen door. Her mom stood at the sink, up to her elbows in soapy water.

"Hi, Mom." Automatically, Miya's eyes swept the room until they found the ugly budget notebook lying on the counter. Miya scowled at it, hating the power the notebook wielded in their lives.

Her mom jumped. "Hey, sleepyhead."

Miya poured a glass of milk. "I can't believe it's almost 10:15. Why didn't you wake me?"

"Oh honey, you've seemed so tired lately. Dad and I decided to let you sleep in. He fed the horses and dogs. I've already taken care of the chickens and gathered the eggs. And speaking of eggs, do you want a couple of eggs and some toast?" Mom turned back to the dishes.

"Maybe later." Miya sipped her milk. *Should I take Jake's advice and mention this dumb anxiety thing to Mom? Having her help rather than those serious-looking counselors on YouTube might be a relief.*

After balancing a pan precariously on top of the dishes in the drainer, her mom said, "I have to run into work for a couple of hours today."

"But it's Saturday." Miya grabbed a dish towel. She rescued the pan from its perch, dried it, and placed it in the cupboard where it belonged.

"Don't remind me," her mom said, pointing skyward. "Mr. Ferguson wants the whole team to meet face to face." Her voice deepened. "Knee to knee. To communicate, work out our differences as cherished employees of the Ferguson team." She glanced at the clock. "And all that fun starts soon."

Although Miya laughed, she wished she had gotten up earlier when her mom drank her first cup of coffee. Things were calmer in the morning. Now, Miya had to share her mom's attention with dishes, Mr. Ferguson, and who knows what else, but it was certainly worth the effort. "I've been worried about some stuff lately."

The dishwater gurgled down the drain. Mom began wiping down the counters. She tossed the dishrag into the sink, opened the refrigerator, and pulled out a plate of chicken and a bag of celery. "Worried about stuff? Like what?"

"Just stuff." Miya stopped, searching for words.

Chop, chop, chop. Mom pushed the celery toward her. "Here, throw this in the crock pot." She headed toward the pantry for an onion. "Worried? I know how you feel."

Miya dumped the celery on top of the chicken. She watched her mom come back and attack the onion. Eyes watering from the onion's sharp bite, Mom looked at the clock again. "Eleven o'clock. I've got to be out of here by noon." She swiped her eyes with the back of her hand. "What were you saying?"

"Oh…nothing much. I'll figure it out." Miya opened the screen door. "Guess I'll go for a ride. An easy one before our barrel run tonight."

Mom chopped faster. "I'd forgotten you were up, but we can still make it work."

"Make what work?"

"The Kemplers' garage sale, remember? We need to support them. Meet me here at three. We can run over there and back before supper."

Miya's heart dropped. The Kempler sale. It was too depressing to think about. At that moment, the sink gurgled again. Miya thought about a hot pot in Yellowstone.

"Ahh!" Miya's mom threw the onion down on the cutting board and sprinted to the sink. "Don't you *dare* back up on me again!"

Miya eased out of the kitchen, closing the screen door quietly behind her.

Listening to the sound of boots, Zoey bounded around the side of the house and leaped up onto the porch. Miya dropped to one knee and scratched the collie under the chin. "How are you today, you good, smart, beautiful girl?"

Zoey's tail thumped against the wooden planks as she tilted her head so Miya could reach all the right places. "Want to go for a ride?"

With a yip of excitement, Zoey scampered down the porch steps. She stopped and looked over her shoulder. Zoey barked a second time, then darted a few yards down the path toward the barn. She paused to look back at Miya—whining and smiling a dog smile, one black ear standing straight up, the other folded against her head.

"I'm coming. I'm coming." Miya hitched up her jeans and tightened her belt a notch. A mountain bluebird hopscotched from the lilac bush to a fence post and onto the top of the woodpile.

The sunshine warmed Miya as she stepped off the porch. She stopped, savoring it. Her eyes skipped over the foothills to the top of the mountain, where new snow dusted the canyons and swirled in the shadows. Zoey darted a few more yards toward the barn, then circled back to Miya. The collie flopped down and looked up at her, almond eyes bright with anticipation. "I won't stop anymore. I promise."

With a gleeful bark, Zoey dashed on ahead to the tack room. When Miya caught up, she grabbed the doorknob and pulled hard. The warped door made a scraping sound as it opened across the porch. It needed to be taken off, sanded, and rehung, but Miya knew that was far down the list of Dad's priorities.

The alfalfa cubes were stored in a large metal trashcan. Miya removed the lid and grabbed a few cubes. She lifted the bridle from a hook and hung it over her shoulder. Back outside, Miya saw the horses grazing at the far end of the field. She put two fingers in her mouth, sucked in a deep breath, and whistled. The shrill notes hung in the air. Dream and Hank looked in her direction. Then, they lowered their heads and continued to eat.

"They're ignoring us," Miya said to Zoey. She stuck her fingers in her mouth and blew again, puffing out her eyes and cheeks. This time, Dream strolled toward the barn.

"Come on, girl. Come on, Dream." Miya climbed through the fence and held out the cubes. Dream began to trot—her strides long and graceful. Miya shook her head, remembering how the paint had bucked her off the first time she'd ridden her. It had taken months to work things out between them, but it had all been worthwhile. Now, she and Dream had come so far that they could almost read each other's thoughts.

When Dream reached Miya, the paint stretched out her neck and nibbled the cubes. Her whiskers tickled Miya's palm. She scratched Dream's wide forehead, where a small piece of sagebrush was tangled in her mane. She worked it free, then stood still as the breeze played across her cheeks. Dream muzzled Miya's shirt, looking for more cubes. "Sorry, that's all for now." She gave the mare a final pat. "We're going for a ride."

She slipped the bridle on Dream, opened the gate, and looked around for Zoey. Her dog stood beside a prairie dog hole, staring at it as though by wishing hard enough, the prairie dog would appear.

"C'mon, Zoey. He probably escaped out the other end and is long gone by now." Zoey woofed and bounded after Miya, crawling under the barbed wire instead of going through the gate. Miya jumped on Dream and turned her toward the trail along the creek.

Rippling water bounced over rocks and boulders. A crow cawed. A doe lifted her head and watched from the willows. Miya allowed Dream to choose her own pace. The mare picked her way over roots and across fallen logs.

Miya visualized storing each of her problems in a box, slamming the lid down, and pushing it all to the far corners of her mind. Her anxiety, the track team girls, and the Kempler Ranch sale were all stored, and a heavy padlock locked each box. After a few miles, Miya's neck and shoulders relaxed.

In a small meadow alongside the creek, Miya sat on the paint while the horse grazed. Lulled by the quiet swish of Dream's tail and the song of the water, Miya lay down on Dream's back. She stared at the sky and made cloud pictures like she used to when she was little. A duck. A Christmas tree. A fish leaping out of the water.

A soft breeze lifted the bangs off Miya's forehead. Dream took baby steps as she munched on the tender grass while Zoey dozed in the shade. Miya closed her eyes and breathed in the smell of the sagebrush, wet leaves, and damp earth.

Gradually, the wind picked up, and the trees creaked. Like mice stealing into a tent and nibbling around the edges of a granola bar, Miya's worries nosed their way out of the boxes. *How bad is the money situation? Will this be the year they lose the ranch?*

Miya leaned forward and hugged Dream. She couldn't bear the thought of the mare being sold. Last weekend, the bank liquidated the Kempler Ranch and auctioned the property to a developer. After almost everything in the house and barns was sold, bidding began on all the livestock.

She twisted the ends of her reins. "If Dad lets me take the rich guy fishing, he might refer a bunch of other rich people. It would be nice not to worry about the ranch."

A cloud sailboat drifted overhead, followed by a cloud ice cream cone and a cloud train. "Maybe we could even take a vacation."

Last year, Aurora's and Brinley's families vacationed together, and the girls made sure everyone knew they had swum with the dolphins in Jamaica and skied in Vail.

"I'd be happy to spend a day at a real amusement park," Miya told Dream. "The best ride I've ever been on is the creaky old Zipper at the fair."

Dream shifted and shook her head at a fly. "I know, there's this thing about keeping my courage up to ride over the pass. I'm pretty sure I can do it. All those people on YouTube have anxiety and still manage to live their lives. I bet some of them have ridden a roller coaster."

Miya straightened her shoulder and her resolve. She turned Dream toward the barn. "C'mon, Dream. Let's go home, meet Mom, and convince Dad. Time to face the music."

Chapter Seven

Miya held two loaves of apple nut bread as her mom pulled up to the front of the Kemplers' house. She exited the car slowly and nudged the door closed with her hip. Ants crawled among the petunias in the flowerbed, shredding the drooping petals.

In the driveway, five plastic tables displayed a variety of used household goods. Mismatched dishes, chipped cups, lamps without shades, faded prints of cowboys riding bucking horses. Beside the last table sat a sagging couch and a stained recliner.

Jennifer Kempler rounded the tables and hugged Miya's mom. "Thank you for coming." Jennifer gestured toward the tables. "This is all that's left after the dispersal sale."

Dispersal sale. Miya hated those words. Why didn't they call it "End of a Dream Sale" or "Let's Take Advantage of Someone Else's Bad Luck Sale?"

Miya's mom looked around. "Where's Jeff?"

"In town, interviewing for a trucking job. He hopes to have something before we have to move out. The stress of job hunting is getting to him," Jennifer said.

Meanwhile, a large lady wearing orange flip-flops and green polyester shorts held up a fleece jacket. "This says a dollar. Will you take fifty cents for it?"

"Sure." Jennifer made a tired shooing gesture with her hand before turning back to Miya and her mom. "I'd better get over there."

"Of course," said Mom. "I'll put the apple bread in your kitchen."

"Thanks for the goodies and for stopping by. Maybe we can get together sometime after we move to town."

Before Miya's mom could reply, the polyester shorts lady yelled, "I only have a quarter and a few pennies. Will that be enough?"

Miya didn't wait to hear Jennifer's answer. She plodded toward the swing set. She couldn't bear to see the Kemplers' livelihood reduced to haggling over a quarter.

Six-year-old Adalita Kempler sat on a cracked plastic swing of a rusty swing set. She held Baby Shark, her pet duck, in her lap. Baby Shark had a deformed foot, which prevented him from walking. Every morning, Adalita carried the duck to the pond, and every evening, she carted him back to the chicken coop, where he'd be safe from predators.

Miya eased down on the swing beside her. Hearing sniffling, she looked more closely at Adalita. "Are you crying?"

"Yes. You'd be crying, too, if you were in my shoes. Momma says Baby Shark has to go with the chickens when the man comes."

The chain of the swing bit into Miya's palm as her hand tightened around it. "Baby Shark? No way!"

"Yep. Momma says there's no room, and he won't be happy in town."

Miya jumped up, the swing flying out behind her. "Give him to me," she said, holding out her arms. "I'll take him home until we convince your mom and dad to let you have him back."

Adalita considered this for a long minute. "What if your momma won't let you take him home?

"She will. Mom loves all animals, but to prove it to you, let's go ask her."

Miya found her mom sitting in the car, staring at the Kemplers' old farmhouse.

"Mom, can we take Baby Shark home with us?" She explained the situation. "Adelita's duck is welcome at our house until the Kemplers have room, right?"

Mom climbed out of the car and knelt before Adalita. She gathered the girl and the duck into her arms. "Of course, Baby Shark is welcome. Especially since Miya is willing to assume full responsibility for her care. Right, Miya?" Mom shot her a meaningful look.

"I'll take good care of him. I promise. Cross my heart."

"I guess it's okay then." With a heavy sigh, Adalita handed Baby Shark to Miya. She kissed the feathers on the top of the duck's head and wiped her eyes with the bottom of her T-shirt.

"Thanks, Miya. Bye, Baby Shark." Adalita's head drooped as she dragged her feet along the path toward the crowd sifting through the family's belongings.

In the car on the way home, Miya thought about the ugly green budget notebook and the constant worry in her mother's eyes. Miya pictured her family's things scattered out on rickety tables while strangers pawed through them. She imagined the pressed flower pictures her mom crafted, her dad's trophy buckles, and the pine desk her uncle Jimmie had made especially for her—all tossed to the wind or, even worse, the county dump.

"There won't be a dispersal sale on our ranch, will there?"

Mom glanced out the window and took a deep breath before answering. "Of...of course not."

Miya didn't believe her. Cradling Baby Shark to her chest, Miya thought about how she hadn't climbed the ladder in the hay loft yesterday. She'd tried the breathing exercises the lady on the video recommended. After giving herself a pep talk, Miya managed four steps up the ladder before getting dizzy. On her way down, Miya closed her eyes and felt for each rung of the ladder with her toe before carefully easing down and committing to the next step.

Today, she'd force herself to climb up five steps, and tomorrow maybe six. Little by little, she'd push herself to feel better. She needed to be ready when her dad agreed to the trip.

At the rodeo that evening, Miya rode Dream around the outside of the warmup area. Laying her reins on Dream's neck, Miya stuffed her hands into her jacket pockets. Other horses passed her, hooves thudding as they trotted or loped by. Ropers swung their ropes, barrel racers chatted in groups of two or three, and the clown's mini donkey brayed as he waited for his cue.

Miya needed to focus on the barrel race—she owed it to Dream. Yet she could only think about the sad collection of belongings in the Kemplers' dusty front yard. Miya stopped her mare and slid off. She tightened the cinch and repositioned Dream's splint and bell boots.

"Hey."

Startled, Miya jumped. She'd been so lost in her thoughts she hadn't heard Jake walk up behind her. "What are you doing here? Why aren't you getting warmed up? What's wrong?"

Jake put a hand on Miya's arm. "Slow down. Nothing's wrong. I saw you and wanted to say good luck and ask how the talk with your mom went."

"It was okay." Miya's face grew warm. She hated lying to Jake, even by omission. "My mom said she can pretty much relate to worrying."

Jake smiled. "That's great, Miya. You can tell me more later. Good luck on your run."

Miya forced herself to return the smile. "Thanks. Good luck to you, too." Miya put her foot in her stirrup and mounted Dream. "I'd better keep warming up, and you'd better get over there." She nodded toward the chutes. "Remember, I'm riding home with Dad tonight, so I can talk to him about the trip."

Miya squeezed her legs, and Dream trotted away.

Fifteen minutes later, the announcer called for the barrel racing to start. Miya and Dream joined the other contestants at the end of the alley. A few of the horses waited calmly, ears pointed toward the arena. Most of the barrel horses jigged in small circles—their muscles bunched, impatient to sprint down the alley.

As usual, Miya's dad came to wait with her until her name was called.

He rubbed Dream on the shoulder, then patted Miya's knee. "Ready to run?"

Miya shifted in her saddle, unable to get comfortable. "I think so." She unwrapped two rubber bands from her saddle horn and handed them to Dad. He positioned the bands around Miya's boot and underneath her stirrups. She was glad the dark shadows hid the hole in her boot. Her dad didn't need to add that to his list of worries.

Peering up at her face, he asked, "Nervous?"

Miya nodded, wishing she could tell him that her barrel run was only the first of many things she was nervous about.

"Just take a deep breath. You and Dream are going to do great."

Her dad bent down and checked Dream's splint boot. *Riiip.* He pulled the Velcro loose on the left front boot, repositioned it, and readjusted the other front boot.

Miya clenched her jaw. She'd already checked Dream's splint boots. They'd been fine.

The announcer called out the times as the girls and their horses swept up and down the alley. "17.3, 17.60, 17.08…" Miya usually didn't listen to the times of the others. She'd learned it was best to focus on doing her own job well, but tonight, the numbers rattled around in her head. The times were fast for this huge arena. Miya and Dream had run a 17.04 here on their best night—when every-thing had been perfect for her and Dream.

Dream danced on her tiptoes, barely able to contain her enthu-siasm—ears pricked forward, muscles tense.

Miya patted her on the neck. "I know you love this but calm down. We're not up till the end."

Slipping off her jacket, Miya handed it to her dad—another lesson she had learned the hard way. She'd lost a barrel race once because the front of her jacket hooked over the saddle horn.

The night wind streamed down from the mountains and wafted through the canyon. Miya hunched forward in her saddle, drawing her shoulders up toward her ears.

"You're almost up." Dad ran his fingers under Dream's cinch, checking for tightness. He nodded, then stepped back. "Good luck, and have fun."

"Thanks." Miya pushed her cowgirl hat down on her head so it wouldn't blow off.

"Next up, Miya Skippingbird on Dream," called the announcer.

Since the wind was buffeting the speakers, it was hard for Miya to hear the announcer's voice, but Dream heard her name and charged down the alley. Miya sat back, signaling Dream to slow down. The mare needed to conserve her energy for the race. The clock hadn't started yet. But as they crossed the electric eye, Miya was out of position, sitting back in her saddle instead of forward.

Dream flattened her ears against her head, stretched out her neck, and dashed down the arena. Before Miya knew it, Dream was near the first barrel. Miya miscalculated and asked her to rate or slow down to turn the barrel too early. Then, Dream slowed down, sped up, and took forever to round the barrel.

Miya spent the few seconds between the first and second bar-rels trying to position Dream to make a decent turn. Despite her best efforts, Dream swung too wide. Miya knew the seconds were ticking by.

The red, white, and blue third barrel sat directly in their path. Miya cued Dream to move over, but it was too late. *Bam!* Miya's shin connected with the lip of the hard plastic barrel, sending a jolt of pain through her leg. The barrel teetered in slow motion. Miya reached out to grab it, but her hand slid off the edge, and the barrel fell to the ground. Miya's cheeks burned. She closed her eyes as Dream loped home.

The announcers voice cut the night air like a hot knife in butter. The speakers resounded unusually loud and clear. "22.3 plus the ten for knocking over a barrel. Miya Skippingbird's total time is 32.31. That's a bit of tough luck for this fine cowgirl. Let's give her a round of applause."

Miya cringed. She didn't want sympathy applause. She wanted out. Out of this arena. She trotted to the gate and stared at the top rail, waiting for the gateman to open it. The gateman, a tall kid in a black cowboy hat, had his arm around a girl in a low-cut tank top. Miya couldn't help but notice he whispered something in her ear and she giggled in response.

Dream pawed the dirt and shook her head, anxious to trot back to the trailer.

"Excuse me? Could you open the gate, please?"

The gateman turned away as his girlfriend slipped her hand into his back pocket. Miya clenched and unclenched her fists, then blew out a frustrated breath. After asking Dream to step parallel to the gate, Miya reached for the latch to let herself out. When the gateman finally spotted her waiting there, he pulled away from the girl and shoved the gate open.

"Thanks." Miya wanted to tell him to do his job instead of acting like a slacker, but that was too much of an effort on her part. Instead, she rode into the shadows.

Miya guided Dream to a darkened spot along the arena fence— away from everyone else. She wished she could return to the horse trailer and cry, but the right thing to do was watch the bull riding and support Jake.

Miya replayed the miserable run in her mind. The entire catastrophe was all her fault. She should have had her head on straight and helped Dream instead of overriding her and getting in her way.

Miya stared down at Dream's mane as hoofbeats approached. She hoped that whoever it was would keep riding by, but the hoofbeats stopped next to her. From the corner of her eye, Miya saw Aurora and Brinley riding double. Miya assumed some besotted cowboy had loaned them his horse to ride around the grounds for a little while.

"Hi, Miya," Brinley spoke in a singsong voice. "Is there room beside you to watch Jake's ride?"

"I guess." Miya's answer fell flat.

She lifted her head to study the pair. Although, in her eyes, their outfits were ridiculous, Miya knew they were also ridiculously expensive. Brinley paired her short shorts with red boots fringed on the sides. Aurora's outfit consisted of a clingy black T-shirt that read NOT MY FIRST RODEO and jean shorts. She topped off the outfit with a turquoise straw hat. The kind of hat that tourists spend way too much money on.

Giggling, the girls maneuvered the bay horse to the fence beside Miya. "We saw your run," said Aurora. "Did you come in last, or did someone else knock over two barrels instead of one?"

Miya fought to keep her face expressionless. *I may have come in last, but I'm a lot faster than people who sit on the sidelines.*

She didn't bother to vocalize the response. What was the use? She knew the pair would twist anything she said, so Miya would appear dumb and defensive. From experience, Miya knew nothing caused more misery than popular girls and their social media accounts.

"Oh, look! There's Jake." Aurora pointed her phone toward the arena.

Jake's spotted bull, Mad Money, took one jump out, spun to the left, and threw him off. Jake sprinted to the fence while the bullfighters distracted the bull.

"Sorry, Jake," Miya whispered under her breath. "You're having a bad night, too."

Backing the bay up, Aurora snickered and said, "Come on, Brin. Let's go console Jake."

Scowling, Miya watched the two girls ride away. She didn't have time to console Jake. She'd text him later. Right now, Miya needed to take care of her horse and meet her dad in the parking lot.

Chapter Eight

In the cab of the truck, Miya jerked her boots off and slumped against the seat. Dad signaled to change lanes before glancing at her. "You want to talk about your run?"

"Not really. It was my fault. I didn't have my mind on it."

Dad nodded. He reached over and squeezed her hand. "You'll do better next time."

Miya loved that Dad understood. Some of her friends had parents who threw fits if their kid didn't win. Miya squeezed his hand back. "Thanks, Dad."

Traffic thinned as they left town. Miya looked out the window and rehearsed, for the twentieth time, all her arguments to persuade her dad to let her lead the fishing trip. Miya unbuckled her seatbelt, shrugged off her jacket, and buckled up again. Nervously, she tapped her stockinged foot up and down on the floorboard.

She took a deep breath, swallowed, and took another deep breath. They passed a row of crooked mailboxes and the Anderson's calving shed. The old truck and trailer rumbled over the first cattle guard. Miya's stomach churned. They were almost home, and she hadn't found her courage yet. Miya clasped her hands in her lap. She closed her eyes and pictured herself lying on Dream's wide back by the creek—the sun warming her face, a gentle breeze stroking her cheeks. Miya counted to twenty and opened her eyes.

"Dad, can we talk?"

"Sure." He angled the truck over the second cattle guard. He watched his sideview mirror to make sure the trailer didn't scrape the posts along the sides.

"I want to talk about the pack trip."

Dad sighed and shook his head. Before he could open his mouth, Miya rushed on. "I know you said I couldn't take it. Just please tell me the reasons why."

Miya's dad looked at her. "All right. After this talk, the case is closed. Agreed?"

"Umm—"

After checking the trailer again, he spoke. "Okay, here goes. It's simple. I need the horses, equipment, truck, and trailer for my trip. So, if I take everything with me, that leaves you with nothing. Can't do a pack trip with nothing."

"Ye-ah." Miya drew the word out into two syllables. She smiled to herself, knowing that she had that obstacle handled. "I agree."

"Plus, you're too young. I'm not sending you up there alone with people I don't know."

"I get that part, Dad. What else?" There was no point in arguing. Age was the one variable over which she had no control.

Squinting through the bug spatter on the windshield, Dad eased the truck into the first of two gigantic potholes. "I don't like the guy. Feels off. He was pretty full of himself on the phone. I get the impression that he's one of those people who solve all their problems by throwing money at them."

Miya braced her hand on the seat as Dad eased the truck through the pothole. "Dad, will you please hear me out? I know I'm only fifteen, but... you don't think I can do anything right." Miya spit her last words out in rapid fire. She paused and drew in a deep breath. "You won't even let me hook up the horse trailer or put on Dream's splint boots without double-checking me." Miya stopped and swallowed her bitterness. Getting mad wouldn't help convince her dad. After a few seconds, she continued. "But I have a plan—a good one."

Miya crouched in the stickers and weeds underneath Dad's office window. A grasshopper popped up and smacked her arm. Miya watched it land in the dirt with a plop before hopping away to another patch of weeds. She stood up cautiously and peeked in the window. Dad was on the phone. His back to her.

She closed her eyes to listen better. She needed to hear every word of this conversation.

"There might be a way we can work something out for those dates. My fifteen-year-old daughter, Miya, her friend, Jake, and his mother will guide you."

There was a pause. Miya held her breath.

"All right," Dad said. "I'll have my lawyer draw up an agreement with these terms. First, Skippingbird Outfitters is not liable if anything happens on this trip."

Silence. Her dad bristled at something the man said. "Then the deal's off. You've read my reviews. You know we do everything in our power to keep clients safe. But you must also understand the risk involved whenever someone rides into the wilderness. If we guide you, you need to be willing to accept that risk, for you and your son."

Miya recognized that tone in her father's voice. There'd be no negotiating about the liability thing. She slumped against the wall. That was it. The deal was off.

Her dad's voice drifted out the window. "Yes, you're right. Jake's mother will ride along, and chances are nothing will go wrong. So, let's start with this. Come out today, meet my daughter, and pay the entire amount in advance. We'll take it from there."

Miya stood up. *Maybe the deal isn't off. Weird, though.* Clients always paid a deposit and settled up on the day of the trip. Miya wondered if her dad had created all these stipulations so this guy would get mad and find someone else to take him fishing.

"No, I won't email it. I'd like to meet you and your son in person. Come out after six, and we'll talk tonight."

Silence. Seconds later, footsteps approached the window. Her dad leaned out. "Why are you hanging out here in the weeds instead of your usual spot?" He smiled and winked. "Looks like you might be taking a pack trip."

Sheepishly, Miya smiled back. "Thanks for trusting me, Dad. I'll keep everything under control. You won't regret this. I promise."

"I hope not." Her dad frowned. "I'm still not entirely comfortable with this Parker guy. Remember, we're canceling if things don't go well tonight." He closed the window.

Miya patted her thighs, so Zoey jumped into her lap for some attention. "Miya Skippingbird, fishing guide. It has a nice ring, doesn't it, Zoey?"

After shoving all her worries about the granite walls and steep cliffs into a box and affixing two strong padlocks, Miya felt a little better. "Everything is going to work out. I'll keep practicing. Tomorrow, I'll make it all eleven steps up into the hay loft before I chicken out. I can do that. Right, Zoey?"

While waiting for Mr. Parker on the front porch, Miya watched Baby Shark splash in his new plastic kiddie pool. She tossed a diving ring in the water. Miya wished she could teach Baby Shark to fetch for Adalita, but the duck didn't seem interested.

"Go get it, Baby Shark." Miya encouraged him.

Baby Shark swam to the opposite side of the pool and stuck his head under his wing.

"Come on, you can do it. Fetch!"

Without waiting for an invitation, Zoey jumped into the pool, nosed the ring against the side, and grasped the purple toy with her teeth. She hopped out of the pool and laid the ring at Miya's feet.

Just as a red SUV pulled up in front of the porch, Zoey shook— spraying droplets of water all over Miya's clean shirt and jeans.

"Zoey, this is not the look I had in mind to meet my first client," Miya said through clenched teeth.

She checked her phone. The Parkers were forty-five minutes late. That wasn't going to impress her dad.

After the SUV parked, the back door flew open. "I'm here!" a thin boy with oversized black glasses announced. "I'm so excited to ride horses!"

Miya wiped the duck water from her cheeks and dried her hand on the thigh of her jeans. "Hi, I'm Miya, and I'm always excited to ride them, too."

The driver's door opened, and a man in his late thirties got out, stretched, and turned in a slow circle. The bottoms of his skinny jeans disappeared into new-looking hiking boots. His eyes flickered over Miya as he hung his sunglasses on the neck of his snow-white T-shirt.

"Your road is impossible."

Miya stopped smiling. She knew how bad the road was and how expensive it was to fix.

Miya borrowed her mom's line. "Keeps away the bill collectors and the faint of heart." She hoped that would put an end to the conversation. Besides being late, Mr. Parker's attitude would provide the perfect excuse for Dad to cancel the trip. Before Mr. Parker could reply, the front door opened. Dad stepped out of the doorway.

"Hi, I'm Michael Skippingbird." Her dad crossed the porch, holding out his hand.

"Dustin Parker." The two men shook hands. "What time do you want us to be here on Saturday?"

Michael stepped back. "Wait a minute. First things first. I want to make sure we're one hundred percent clear. If you come back on Saturday, you need to be on time. If you agree with everything we talk about today, you can sign the paperwork and write a check."

Mr. Parker bristled. "You mean I drove all the way out here—"

"And you can drive all the way back," Michael finished the man's thought and reached for the doorknob.

Miya dashed up the porch steps and touched her dad's arm. "Wait, Dad."

"Yes, wait." Mr. Parker ran a hand through his highlighted hair. "This trip is important to my son, Tanner. Let's talk."

Miya's dad looked at her, then Tanner. Finally, he nodded to Mr. Parker. "All right. In my office."

Miya tried to follow Mr. Parker into the house, but Dad stopped her at the door.

"Why don't you show Tanner the horses while Mr. Parker and I visit?"

"But Dad…" Her dad cut her off.

"Take Tanner to the corral, Miya."

Miya frowned. She knew better than to argue when Dad spoke in that tone of voice, yet this was supposed to be her trip. If she were going to make a perfect plan for the next four days, Miya needed to know what the two were discussing, but she couldn't exactly stand under the office window while Tanner waited for her.

As the screen door slammed behind the two men, Miya forced herself to smile at the boy. "C'mon. I have a package of chocolate chip cookies here, so let's go meet Dollar."

Ten minutes later, Miya leaned her forehead on the corral fence and put her boot on the bottom rail. Tanner imitated her. His pale legs stuck out from navy blue athletic shorts. He wore an oversized gray T-shirt with OWL CREEK CAMP written across the back. The sleeves reached almost to his elbows, and when he pointed at Dollar, Miya noticed a superhero band-aid on the inside of his arm.

"Did you get hurt?"

Tanner pulled his arm back and held it against his side. "No, the nurse gave me a shot for my allergies and stuff."

Miya turned her attention back to Dollar—a short, wide pony the color of a mud fence and, in Miya's opinion, just as ugly. His tail was crooked, his long ears flopped as he meandered around the corral, and his coat was as rough as a steel wool pad. On the positive side, however, Dollar was as sure-footed as a mountain goat and always brought his rider home safely.

Miya pointed at Dollar. "There's your horse."

"Wow, he's beautiful. Is he nice?"

"Most of the time. Sometimes Dollar likes to sneak back to the trailer from camp at night. And if you're not paying attention, he'll play a few tricks on you."

Tanner stepped back from the fence. "What kind of tricks?"

"If he gets sweaty, he likes to lay down and roll in a sandy spot on the trail."

Miya didn't mention how Dollar also liked to walk under tree limbs if his rider wasn't paying attention. When she'd been day-dreaming one time, Dollar dragged her under a few. Tanner smiled at the brown pony slurping water from the trough.

"He won't do that to me. He'll be good. Why did you name him Dollar?"

"I didn't. My dad did. He jokes around a lot and offered to pay anyone a dollar who would take him home."

Tanner's eyes lit up. "I will!"

Miya climbed through the fence. "You better get to know him before you make any offers. Ready to say hello?"

Tanner didn't move. His eyes darted from Dollar to Miya and back again. "Is it safe?"

"We'll be fine. We'll catch him, and you can feel how soft his muzzle is."

Instead of climbing through the rails, Tanner squatted and crawled under the fence. He stood up and dusted off his knees. Miya took two cookies out of the package. She gave one to Tanner. "Dollar would rather have homemade, but Chips Ahoy will do in a pinch. Follow me."

Miya held out a cookie to Dollar. He trotted toward her, his long tail nearly touching the ground. Dollar took the cookie in his yellow teeth and munched on it, his head nodding up and down.

Tanner approached Dollar with the cookie in his outstretched hand. Dollar finished the first cookie and swung his head around toward Tanner.

"Oh no." Tanner stumbled backward. "He's looking at me!"

"No worries. He hasn't eaten any kids in a long time."

"Very funny." Tanner's mouth turned up at the corner.

Dollar looked expectantly at Tanner.

"Hold your cookie out flat."

When Dollar's lips touched Tanner's palm, Tanner jerked back, and the cookie fell to the ground.

Miya bent down and rescued the cookie. "Try again. Give him a chance. He won't bite you."

"But he tickled me."

"I know, but you can't jerk away. How would you feel if someone offered you a candy bar but grabbed it back before you took a bite?"

Tanner braced his feet a little wider and cautiously held out his palm. Dollar accepted the cookie, swallowed it in two bites, and gazed hopefully at Tanner for another.

"I fed Dollar all by myself!" Tanner beamed.

"You did. Let's feed him a couple more, and he'll be your friend forever."

As Miya reached into the package, Mr. Parker appeared and shouted, "It's time to go, Tanner."

Without turning, Tanner said, "In a minute. We're feeding chocolate chip cookies to Dollar."

Mr. Parker rattled the gate. "*Now.* We're late. You can feed him when we come back."

Tanner sighed. "We wouldn't be late if Dad hadn't been soooo busy at his office, and now we have to rush off because... surprise—he's late for something again."

"What did you say?" Mr. Parker demanded as he fiddled with the gate latch.

"Nothing."

Miya put the cookies back in the package. "Your dad did say you were coming back. That's the important thing. You better go now, and we'll feed Dollar next time."

"I guess." Tanner shrugged. "Bye, Dollar. Bye, Miya." He scooted under the fence and scuffed up the path behind his dad, kicking up rocks and dirt.

Chapter Nine

Miya stood in the middle of one of the Runningdeers' sheds, clipboard in hand. Jake set a pair of canvas panniers on the floor.

"That's the last of the stuff in the loft. I think you have everything now."

Miya surveyed the boxes of camping gear, pack saddles and pads, tents, and tools. "I hope so. Thanks for getting it all down for me."

Jake opened a tub and took out a hard plastic box. He flipped open the case. "Don't forget this. Dad makes sure our subscription is always paid up."

Miya took the green and black device from Jake. They wouldn't have cell service at Wildcat Falls, but if an emergency arose, they could use this Inreach to text for help.

"Thanks. I'll put it in my saddle bag."

Jake nodded. "Do you need some help sorting all this out?"

"Nope. My trip. My responsibility. Besides, you'll distract me, and I need to stay super organized and on top of things."

Jake stepped back, holding up his hands, palms toward her. "Okay. Okay."

Miya laid her clipboard on top of a tub labeled POTS AND PANS.

"Sorry. I know you mean well, and I appreciate it. But if you start helping, little by little you'll take over, and it won't be my trip anymore."

A wasp buzzed through the open door and landed on the spout of a coffee pot. Jake took off his ball cap and scratched his head.

"Miya, I don't want to take over, and no one ever said it wasn't your trip." Another wasp flew in and disappeared inside the coffee pot.

"Mr. Parker did. I mean, he didn't actually come out and say it," Miya moved away from the coffee pot, "but you should have seen when he came out to the house. He never even so much as gave me the time of day except to criticize the road."

Miya studied the scuff mark on the toe of her boot. "He'll think your mom is in charge cuz she's old, or you're in charge cuz you're a *guy*." Miya made air quotes with her fingers around the word "guy."

"And me? I'm just the babysitter."

Jake pulled Miya into a hug. After a minute, she allowed herself to relax against him.

"I think you're overreacting. Even if Mr. Parker doesn't act like you're in charge, we know the truth. That's what's important."

They stood quietly for a few seconds as the wasps buzzed against the sides of the metal pot.

Jake spoke into her hair. "How is the anxiety thing going?"

Miya stiffened. "Okay."

"I can't believe your mom told you to ignore it."

Miya hid her face in Jake's shirt so he wouldn't see she was lying. A twinge of guilt sat heavy on her conscience. Truth be told? She hadn't brought it up with Mom again because her mom would tell Dad. With all his doubts, this would push him over the edge. He'd cancel the trip.

"Um...she didn't really say 'ignore it.' She just said to 'face up to it.'"

Jake hugged her tighter. "I hope you're ready to face Wildcat Pass."

Inwardly, Miya winced. In her mind's eye, she saw the beginning of the trail—three feet wide and carved out of red rock. She could handle that. The terrifying part was the granite face of the mountain that bordered one side of the trail and the 500-foot drop-off on the other.

Miya swayed. She forced herself to close her eyes and take several deep breaths. Stepping away from Jake, she said, "I can do it. It's not even that steep compared to some of the other passes."

Jake rubbed his neck. "I know, but—"

"I can do it!"

An awkward silence filled the room until Jake finally spoke. "I know you can do it, Miya. You don't have to face it alone. Mom and I will be there for you."

"You didn't tell your mom about my problem, did you?"

Jake shook his head. "Of course not. That's your story to tell."

"Thanks for keeping my troubles to yourself for a while." Miya leaned against the wall. "I can handle it."

More silence, except for the wind rattling the broken screen in the window. "Maybe you could handle it better by letting other people help you. Especially the ones who care about you."

Miya concentrated on a stain on the floor. Jake left, slamming the door behind him.

The next afternoon Miya tore open a box of instant oatmeal packets and stuffed them into a gallon-size sandwich bag. She surveyed the groceries piled high on the floor. A small bottle of ketchup oozed out from one bag. A box of pancake mix peeked from another. Miya sighed. It would take hours to weigh, measure, and pack all this food.

Skirting the groceries, her mom entered the living room and held out a set of plastic salt and pepper shakers. "I filled these for you."

"Thanks." Miya checked them off the list. "Would you try calling Mr. Parker? I've texted about a hundred times, but he doesn't answer."

"No way, kiddo." Mom shook her head. "Your trip. Your responsibility." She smiled. "Your words."

Miya frowned. She'd used that same phrase with both her mom and Jake. Miya picked up a box of kitchen matches and slid them into a sandwich bag. She sealed the top carefully. "But Mom, Mr. Parker needs to come out so I can give Tanner a riding lesson. And if I can adjust Mr. Parker's stirrups and gear, we can leave the trailhead sooner." Miya used her most pitiful-sounding voice. "Please, Mom."

Her mom shook her head again. "I understand it's hard to talk to people you don't know. I sometimes dread calling clients, but if you want to take the lead on this trip, you have to do it yourself." Mom picked up Miya's phone. "Want me to dial for you?"

Miya grabbed the phone. "No. I'll call when I'm ready."

"Best get it over with." Mom headed back to the kitchen.

Miya stared at the phone. It would probably go to voice mail. She could handle that. Miya composed a message in her mind and scrolled through her contacts. She pressed send.

"Parker here." The voice was curt.

Miya opened her mouth. Closed it. She scanned her brain frantically searching for the prerecorded message she'd rehearsed seconds ago.

"Hello?" A hint of impatience entered his tone.

"Uh, hi." Miya croaked out the words.

"Excuse me?" Mr. Parker's voice was even sharper.

Miya's cheeks burned. The heat reached the tips of her ears. She cleared her throat. "Hello, Mr. Parker. This is Miya Skippingbird."

"Skippingbird?"

"Yes." She shoved a bedroll aside and sat down on the couch. "The one who's leading your pack trip in two days."

"Oh. *The girl*. Right. Is there a problem?"

Miya's foot tapped up and down. The girl.

Rolling her eyes, Miya cleared her throat. "No problem. Could you bring Tanner out tomorrow so I can give him a riding lesson, and while you're here—"

"No, sorry. Too busy. I'm already taking time off for the trip."

Miya's foot bounced up and down. "You can come in the evening. I'd feel much better if Tanner knew the basics before we start down the trail."

"Tanner will pick it up on the way. He'll be sitting on that horse for hours. I'll be there on Saturday. No sooner."

Miya's foot bounced harder. "But..." Before she could get in another word, Mr. Parker hung up.

Miya stared at her phone. How could the man hang up without so much as a goodbye? She texted Jake to tell him how rude Mr. Parker had been.

Hey, sorry again for being so grumpy yesterday. Wanted to tell you about Parker's latest insult. Can you come over tonight?

Jake texted back.

> Can't tonight. Going for a long run. Got to stay in shape for cross country. Tomorrow, okay?

Miya chewed on the eraser of her pencil. She wanted to ask if the run included Aurora or Brinley, but Jake would accuse her of being weird and overreacting. Miya didn't want to start another argument, so she made a face at the phone and texted back.

> Fine. See you tomorrow.

Besides, if Aurora and Brinley ran with Jake, she'd find out soon enough. It would be all over social media by midnight.

Two mornings later, Miya sat up and switched on the bedside lamp. Zoey lay curled in a warm ball against the back of Miya's legs.

The clock read 1:22. Today was the day. The day she would overcome her fears and win her life back. The muscles in Miya's neck knotted. Pain traveled up past the collar of her T-shirt to the base of her skull. It was as though long, bony fingers gripped her neck.

"Ugh." Miya opened the bottle of generic ibuprofen on her nightstand and shook out two. The tablets were so small she didn't bother to get up for a glass of water. She dry-swallowed them and fell back on her pillow. When Miya closed her eyes, the switchbacks on the way to Wildcat Pass loomed in the distance. Acid rose in her throat—she coughed.

"Zoey, I wish I'd never come up with this dumb idea."

Miya forced herself to take a deep breath for five seconds, hold it in for five seconds, and breathe out for five. A sickly sweet smell rose from the lavender cubes in the wax warmer. The lady on YouTube claimed that lavender provided a calming scent. Miya made a face. Her room smelled like her grandma's pajama drawer, so much for the cubes.

Miya got up and unplugged the warmer despite what YouTube had recommended. Her turned-off phone sat on her desk because she refused to sleep with it. The phone beckoned, tempting her to pick it up, but she resisted. She discovered Jake hadn't run with them the other night. Yet, if Miya scrolled through social media now, her mind would spin in an endless loop of worry and frustration. Today, she needed to focus one hundred percent of her energy on making this trip successful.

Miya opened the bottom drawer of her desk and took out her journal. She sketched in the journal daily because she needed her worries to live somewhere other than her head.

Flipping through the pages, Miya studied the sketches. The first drawings were of Dream—not long after the two had almost fallen off the mountain. She turned the pages of the journal slowly.

In one drawing, a troll crouched in the hay loft, leering at her. In another, Jake knelt on the shed roof, pounding nails while a were-wolf snapped at him. A third depicted a zombie driving a pickup on the switchbacks to one of the campgrounds.

Reaching for a Blackwing pencil, Miya rested it lightly in her fingers, enjoying the smooth feel of it. After a few seconds, she flipped to the next page of the journal and started sketching. Forty-five minutes later, Miya examined her picture—a tiny image of herself sitting on Dream. Riders were behind her. In the picture, she studied the pass on an enormous mountain, where monsters lurked in the crevices of the rock, the branches of the trees, and the ripples of the creek.

Miya selected a 2B pencil to add shading. The monsters leaped off the page with each stroke. When she was finished, Miya tucked the journal into her duffel. Carrying her boots, she crept down the stairs. She needed to go over everything on her list—one more time. One last time. There would be no mistakes.

Chapter Ten

Miya stared at her chipped fingernails so she wouldn't have to look out the window. She realized her breath was coming in quick, short gasps. Jake downshifted and drove around a blind corner.

"You okay?"

Miya nodded, not trusting herself to speak. They were on their way to the trailhead. Jake's mom was in the lead, driving the stock trailer. Jake and Miya followed with a four-horse trailer, and Mr. Parker and Tanner followed in the red SUV.

"I don't remember this road being so narrow. I can't stand to look." Miya chewed on her thumbnail. "You're doing a good job driving."

"Thanks." Jake glanced over at her for an instant and smiled. "Keeping the trailer from crossing the yellow line on these tight curves isn't easy."

Miya wished Jake hadn't said that. Worrying about sliding off the side of the mountain was one thing. Being hit head-on by a tourist in an RV was quite another.

When Jake focused again on the road, Miya slipped her hand up to her heart. She closed her eyes and concentrated on sending warmth from her hand into her heart—another trick she had learned from YouTube.

Miya took a deep breath. It was working. She felt warmth, kindness, and her own strength seep into her heart. Her breathing slowed. She felt calmer. She was in control.

To keep her mind off the dizzying heights as they climbed, Miya reviewed the schedule in her head. Mr. Parker and Tanner would mount their horses by 11:00. They'd ride to the lunch spot, arrive at 1:00, spend half an hour eating, and press on toward camp. By 6:00, they'd set up. At 7:00, they'd dine on chili and cornbread for supper, tell a few stories around the campfire, and turn in early. That was the timetable, and Miya vowed to stick to it.

An hour later, they pulled into the trailhead. Miya stuck her head out the window and inhaled the clean mountain air. The smell of warm sun on the pines was her favorite scent in the whole wide world. She opened the door, and as soon as Jake slowed the truck, she popped out.

And just that fast, Mr. Parker stomped toward them, waving his cellphone. Tanner trotted a few feet behind him with a pinched look of worry.

Mr. Parker stuck his phone under Miya's nose. "Took us long enough to get here, and now there's no service." He glared at Miya. "You claim to be a guide. I was under the impression that guides communicate with their clients, especially about the important things—like *cell* service."

Miya stared at him in confusion. She thought everyone understood that mountains block cell signals, but obviously, some people didn't.

"Mr. Parker—"

He impatiently cut her off. "I have important calls to make." Mr. Parker waved his phone at her. "I'm driving back to where I can get service and get ahold of these people." He spoke over his shoulder to Tanner. "You stay here."

Miya blinked in astonishment. Her client just called her a terrible guide, and they hadn't even left the trailhead. She needed to keep Mr. Parker happy so he'd leave good reviews, but the group also needed to get on the trail as soon as possible.

Without another word, Mr. Parker turned and jogged toward his SUV.

"Wait, Dad!" Tanner yelled.

Jolted out of her thoughts, Miya ran after him. "Yes, wait, please!"

Mr. Parker slowed to a fast walk as Miya tried to catch up. "Sorry about the misunderstanding. We're packing up fairly quickly and starting up the trail. We need to make it across Wildcat Pass so we get camp set up before nightfall."

Sighing theatrically, Mr. Parker asked, "So when do *you* want to leave?"

"We'll be ready in an hour and a half." Two hours was more probable, but she mentally built in some wiggle room.

"Depends on how far I have to go to get a signal. I'll try to be back in an hour or so." Mr. Parker reached into the SUV. "Here are my duffels, and here's Tanner's. My fly rods are too expensive to leave with you. You can pack them when I return."

Miya stared at the two fat green duffle bags and the small orange one lying on the ground.

"Mr. Parker, my dad told you everything must be packed in on horses. We don't have room for anything that wasn't on the list he gave you. Remember? The list said *one* duffle apiece."

Mr. Parker shrugged. "You're a smart girl. You'll figure it out." With that, he got into the red SUV and drove away.

"Bye, Dad," Tanner whispered.

Miya clenched her jaw so tightly that her teeth hurt. She picked up the green duffel bags and returned to the trailer. They were heavy. Mr. Parker was going to have to unpack them and leave some items behind. Miya groaned. This would put them on the trail even later.

Miya wanted to kick at a rock in her path, but since Tanner was walking beside her, she restrained herself. Instead, she stared at the green duffel in her right hand. It was a puke green, almost as nasty looking as the cover of the budget notebook.

"Sorry, Miya," Tanner said.

Forcing a smile, Miya said," It's not your fault, besides..."

Before Miya could finish her sentence, Janelle called from the other side of the stock trailer. "Jake, Miya, come over here, would you?"

"What's up?" Jake asked as the three drew closer.

"Take a look at Comet."

Janelle's favorite horse, a tall black mare named Comet, stood with her head down, refusing to put any weight on her back left leg. Instead, the mare rested the tip of her front hoof on the ground.

Miya kissed Comet on the nose and rubbed her forehead. The horse's eyes were dull with pain.

"I think the problem is close to her stifle." Janelle motioned to the kneecap area on Comet's leg.

Jake ran his hand gently down Comet's hind leg. "Yep. It's swollen and warm. She must have gotten kicked in the trailer."

"I gave her some Bute." Janelle pointed to a white tube that sat on the wheel well of the horse trailer. "It will take a little time for the pain reliever to kick in."

Jake and Miya nodded. Comet pushed her nose into Janelle's belly and sighed. Janelle straightened the mare's forelock. With the tip of her finger, she traced the white diamond on Comet's head.

"I'm taking her to the vet." Janelle looked at Jake. "I'll have your dad meet me at the vet's and take over with Comet. I'll go home, catch another horse, and ride after you."

Miya looked over Comet's back at Tanner, who sat in the grass, talking to Dollar. Even though the morning was cool, Miya felt the sweat gather along her spine.

"That should work." Jake touched Comet's back leg again. "It will take us a while to pack up. We'll be on the trail longer since we're riding with dudes. You should pull in late afternoon or early evening. The timing works fine, Mom."

Janelle wiped a smear of white paste off Comet's muzzle. "Bute must taste terrible, but I think it's working. Come on, you guys. Help me load her up."

As the horse trailer pulled away, Miya's heart pounded. Although this was her trip, Miya counted on Janelle to help handle any big emergencies that might crop up. Zoey pushed her nose against Miya's leg.

"I can do it. I know I can," Miya said to Zoey. "And besides, Janelle will be back in a few hours. Only a few hours—"

"Ready, boss?" Jake's brown eyes twinkled as he looked down at her. He nudged her lightly with his hip. "You'll be fine. Do you want me to brush and saddle horses or unload the gear?"

Miya took a deep breath and smiled back at Jake. He was right. She'd be fine. Janelle might be gone for a while, but in the meantime, she and Jake could handle things together.

"Thanks, Jake." Miya unlatched the tack compartment on the trailer. "I'll unload and organize." She removed a large canvas pack cover from the stack and spread it out on the ground. She unloaded the gear, ticking the items off her list one by one.

Tanner wandered over. "How will we get all this stuff up on the mountain?"

Miya pointed to the sets of panniers. "Those are horse suitcases. But we have to pack them carefully so they weigh the same on both sides and nothing rattles. Want to help?"

"Sure." Tanner peered inside a pannier. "Where do we start?"

Three and a half hours later, Jake dozed in the cab of his truck while Miya paced back and forth in front of it. Tanner and Zoey splashed in the creek, chasing minnows.

Jake leaned out the window. "Do you want me to find him?"

Miya climbed into the passenger side so Tanner wouldn't overhear the conversation. "Yes, you'd better go look. If we don't get on the trail in an hour, we'll have to postpone the whole thing until tomorrow."

Miya bit the inside of her cheek. "That means loading everything up, driving miles home, and starting all over again in the morning,"

Jake nodded. "You're right."

"The whole point of Mr. Parker paying us so much was accommodating his time frame, not ours. So, if we have to shorten this trip, I'm not refunding his money. Besides, we've already spent a lot of it."

She exited the truck and slammed the door so hard that it rattled. The red SUV pulled into the trailhead.

"Dad!" Tanner pulled on his boots and sprinted toward the vehicle.

Turning away, Miya said, "C'mon, let's get a couple of panniers up on the horses. I'm too mad to talk to that man right now. I'll tell him to put his important stuff in one duffle in a minute and ask him to bring his precious fly rod over."

Jake grinned. "That little chat ought to be fun."

Miya picked up a neatly coiled lash rope and pack cover. She headed toward the hitching rail where the pack horses were tied without replying.

Mr. Parker intercepted her. "Where's Janelle?"

Miya stopped walking. "Janelle had to take a horse to the vet. She'll meet us in camp."

"Oh. Well, where's Jake?"

Miya dropped the pack cover. It landed with a thud. "Why?"

"I need to discuss a few things with him. Like where to pack my fly rods."

"First of all, let's get a couple of things straight. My dad told you that *I'm* in charge of this trip. Not Jake. Not Janelle. You agreed and even signed a contract." The blood pounded in Miya's ears. "Second, we don't have time to chat. For everyone's safety, we need to push hard, or we'll ride up a steep, rocky trail at night."

Mr. Parker tried to interrupt, but Miya held up a hand. "It's only a quarter moon tonight. That won't give us much light." Miya bent down and picked up the pack cover. "Repack your stuff so you have one duffle. After that, bring one fly rod over."

Miya glared at him and tightened her grip on the pack cover.

"You can't talk to me like that. Of course, I want everyone to be safe. I got a bit delayed. That's part of doing business." Mr. Parker removed his sunglasses and polished them on the bottom of his T-shirt. He put them back on. "However, may I remind you that *you* work for me. And I mean it when I say I need everything in my duffels."

Miya opened her mouth to reply. Before she could say another word, Jake appeared at her side. "If you want to take this trip, Mr. Parker, you need to do exactly what Miya says."

Miya glanced at Jake—so calm and relaxed. She had seen this same easy-going stance right before he got down on a bull or ran out on the floor to salvage a basketball game.

There was a pause as Mr. Parker appraised Jake. A camp robber flew down from a cottonwood tree, cawing loudly. It picked at Tanner's apple core abandoned next to his book.

"Dad." Tanner pulled on Mr. Parker's arm. "You promised."

"I did." He shot Miya a challenging look. "I will agree to leave some of the gear behind, but I insist on taking both fly rods."

Miya wanted to scream in frustration. Instead, she forced herself to nod. "Fine. We'll pack one of the rods on top of the panniers. If the other rod breaks down enough, you can wrap it in your slicker and tie it on the horse behind you."

She turned to Jake. "Let's pack Vista first."

Vista was a roan pack horse with a playful personality. As they turned toward her, Miya watched the horse nibbling at the lead rope with her lips.

"She's pretty good at untying herself." Jake rubbed Vista's shoulder. "So, keep an eye on her."

"Got it." Miya carried one of the panniers of horse feed closer to Vista. She waited while Jake did the same. Miya and Jake each lifted a canvas pannier onto the sawbucks, the two wooden Xs mounted to the top of the saddle. Next, Miya placed a bedroll on the top.

Jake picked up one side of the pack cover. Miya grasped the other side of the large canvas square. She pulled the cover up from behind Vista and over the load, careful not to spook Vista by waving it around. Miya threw the lash rope, a soft rope with a hook on the end, over the top of the pack to Jake. Together, they tied a box hitch.

"Nice." Jake grinned. "That only took about ten minutes."

Miya admired their handiwork. Vista carried a lumpy bundle on both sides covered with beige canvas and secured with a rope.

Miya and Jake turned toward Daisy, the next packhorse. Jake retied Daisy's halter. "Before we go too far, we need Tanner's and Mr. Parker's duffels."

"Right." Miya's headache was back. She rubbed her temples. "I'll get them."

First, she needed a drink. Miya dragged her feet toward Jake's truck and grabbed her water bottle. As she swallowed, she gave herself a pep talk. She would be calm, cool, and collected, just like Jake. Miya closed her eyes briefly. When she opened them, she noticed the Inreach on the truck seat.

Miya grabbed it and headed toward Dream to slip it into the saddlebag. Before she got there, Mr. Parker met her. "Here is my *one* duffle." He tossed it at her feet. Miya ignored the emphasis on the word "one."

"Thanks." Miya held up the Inreach. "Could you take your duffel over to Jake? I'm on my way to put this in my saddlebag."

Mr. Parker took it out of her hand. He flipped on the power switch. "This is certainly old school, but I guess it works."

Miya clenched and unclenched her fists. I will be calm, cool, and collected, she reminded herself.

"Yes, it works."

Mr. Parker turned the device over. "Is it even waterproof?"

Miya snatched the Inreach back. "Probably not. I keep it in a plastic bag in my saddlebag to keep it dry."

"Wait!" Mr. Parker stepped in front of her. "Look at mine. I bought it yesterday, just for this trip." He bent down and unzipped his duffel. He removed a small black and orange rectangular device and handed it to her. "The Explorer. It's waterproof, shockproof, preloaded with topo maps, and has a digital compass, a barometric altimeter—"

Miya's eyes glazed over. She didn't have time to be impressed by toys. "It's nice and light, but can you call for help?"

Mr. Parker looked affronted. "Of course. The SE-SAR monitors it for potential emergencies. Yours is so big and bulky. Why don't we leave yours behind and take mine?"

Miya touched the buttons of the Explorer. It sprang to life with a bright LED display. It would be nice to have a waterproof Inreach. That way, she wouldn't have to worry about the plastic bag leaking. Shockproof was good, too. Things were always getting bumped and banged up around horses.

Miya nibbled on a hang nail. She'd have more room in her saddlebag for the first aid kit and lunches if she didn't have to make room for the bulky Inreach.

"Okay. We'll take yours. But put it in your saddlebag instead of your duffel, so it will be easy to reach if we need it."

Miya worked the wire loop off the top of the Forrest Service post and dragged the gate wide open. As the others rode through, Miya scanned each horse. She allowed herself a small sigh of relief. They had reached the top of the first hill. The packs were centered and balanced, and all the horses and riders seemed content for the moment.

Miya's hand trembled as she shut the gate. She had never celebrated reaching the two-mile mark before, but it was a victory on this ride. She wondered how two people could be so naïve about horses or the mountains. She had to yell "Duck!" when they'd reached the first set of tree limbs. On top of that, Tanner dropped his reins twice, allowing Dollar to stop and graze. Meanwhile, Mr. Parker shook his jacket so hard he spooked the pack horses, causing Vista to break away. Thank goodness Jake had been there to catch the horse and help sort things out.

Running her fingers through Dream's mane, Miya took a deep breath. She could do this. She had to. With extra vigilance, everything would work out fine from now on.

Squaring her shoulders, Miya asked brightly, "Is everyone okay?" She cringed at the false note in her voice. Jake raised his eyebrows, but Tanner didn't notice. He gave her a thumbs up. Mr. Parker merely nodded.

"Good," Miya said. "We'll ride a few more miles before we cross the creek."

Careful not to disturb the grizzly tracks in the soft dirt, Miya mounted Dream. She wasn't about to mention the tracks to the Parkers, but she knew Jake had noticed them. Since no other animal had stepped on top of them, the tracks were fresh—five toes and corresponding claws.

She was glad there was only one set of medium-sized tracks. That meant that it was a single bear, probably a teenage boar. Miya hoped the bear wouldn't appear and spook a horse or scare the Parkers. She comforted herself with the thought that a smart bear would probably slip into the willows and disappear along the creek.

"Hup, Daisy. Hup, Vista." Miya spoke to the pack horses to warn them they were moving off. She touched Dream with her heels, and the group started up the trail toward a sandy-colored flat. A slight breeze ruffled the olive-green leaves of the sagebrush. Bits of wispy clouds floated high in the air as the sun continued across the sky.

Miya eyed the ridges and valleys of the mountain ahead of her. She had almost forgotten Wildcat Pass in the flurry of packing and riding out. But now, fear coiled in the pit of her stomach. "I am strong," she said softly. "I am not afraid." Miya timed the words to Dream's hoof beats. "I am strong. I am not afraid." Miya looked up at the mountain before her and repeated, "I am strong. I am not afraid of heights."

As they approached Wildcat Pass, Miya hoped her words were true.

Chapter Eleven

Miya glanced behind her. At the most, they had traveled another mile, and Dollar had fallen behind again. The pony ambled along, nipping off pieces of tall grass or stopping entirely to graze. The grass stuck out from both sides of his mouth and waved gently as he chewed. When Dollar lifted his head, he "smiled" at Miya in a self-satisfied way.

"I wish I had a whole bag of Snickers," Miya said to Dream. "I would jam three into my mouth because chocolate might be the only thing that can help me deal with Dollar's antics."

Keeping her voice light, Miya said, "Tap him a little bit, Tanner, so he'll stay up. Mr. Chubby is taking advantage of you."

"Okay, Miya." Tanner tapped the heels of his boots against Dollar's sides. Dollar ignored him and wandered off the trail in search of a juicier morsel.

"Doll...ar!" Miya drew his name out. "Come back here."

Dollar turned, heaved a huge sigh, and trotted down the trail to Miya. Tanner bounced in the saddle; his butt smacked the seat with each of Dollar's strides.

"He does that every time we need to catch up, and it hurts," Tanner said.

"Show him who's boss," Mr. Parker said. "If you don't want him to trot, don't let him. End of story."

Tanner slumped in the saddle. "I'm trying."

Miya drummed her fingers on her thigh. She bit back a retort, reminding Mr. Parker that much of this could have been avoided if he had brought Tanner in earlier for a riding lesson.

Instead, Miya spoke to Tanner. "How about this? You tighten up your reins so he can't reach the grass and try your best to keep up. I'll slow down so you don't have to trot as much."

She chewed her bottom lip. If she slowed the pace, getting to camp would take even longer.

"Hang in there, Tanner." Jake's voice came from the back of the string. "I bet Miya has a good story to tell to take your mind off trotting."

"Really?" Tanner asked. "Do you know any scary ones?"

Miya often told stories to her younger cousins on long rides, but she wished Jake hadn't volunteered her today. She wasn't in the mood for storytelling.

Miya rubbed her forehead and said, "Let me think about it a minute. Besides scary stories, what kind of stories do you like?"

"I like Minecraft."

Miya didn't want to talk about Minecraft, ghosts, or vampires. She needed to concentrate on what loomed ahead—Wildcat Pass.

Slap, slap. Miya heard Tanner's rear end bounce against the saddle as Dollar fell into line behind her pack horses. Miya sighed. "I don't know any Minecraft stories, but I could tell you about a friend and her pet duck named Baby Shark."

It was hours past lunch when the group pulled into the lunch spot. Mr. Parker and Tanner dismounted stiffly.

"Hang on to your horses for a second." Miya looped Vista's lead rope once around her saddle horn and started back to Daisy. "As soon as Jake and I tie up our horses, we'll grab yours."

"I'm going to the bushes." Mr. Parker threw his reins over a clump of thorny weeds by the trail.

"Wait for me, Dad." Tanner dropped Dollar's reins and hurried after him.

Jake tied one of his pack horses to a dead tree. "Mr. Parker, do you have your bear spray?"

"Of course I do. In my saddlebag. I bought some just for this trip." Without looking back, Mr. Parker disappeared into the woods.

Jake's mouth quirked. "I should have said, 'Do you have your bear spray *with* you cuz it won't do you a bit of good in your saddlebag.'"

Miya grabbed Dollar's reins. "They should be okay. They're making enough noise to scare away a dozen grizzlies."

After tying up Dream and her pack horses, Miya led Dollar to another tree. "You need to quit being such a slowpoke. We'll never get to camp at this rate." Dollar merely stared at her, blinking his stubby brown lashes.

"Okay. You win. I'm ready to deal. You pick up the pace, and I'll bake you a whole batch of chocolate chip cookies when we get home." Miya knew it was her imagination, but she could have sworn Dollar "smiled."

Jake tied up Crackerjack, Mr. Parker's horse. "Hey, Miya. Good thing Crackerjack decided to stay with his buddies, or Mr. Parker would have had a long walk back."

"Which he deserves." Miya moved over to Dream and opened her saddlebags. She pulled out three snack-size bags of trail mix. "What do you think our odds are of getting to camp by nightfall?"

Jake studied the sky. "It will be close. The way the clouds are moving in, we probably won't have much of a moon to help."

A gust of damp wind lifted the hair off Miya's neck. "Let's hope we get the bedrolls in the tent before it rains."

Mr. Parker and Tanner crashed through the trees close by them. When they stepped out of the clearing, Miya held out the trail mix. "Here's a snack."

"Aren't you having any?" Tanner asked, picking out the raisins. "I don't like these, but I'll see if Dollar does."

"He might eat them," Miya said, "but he'd probably rather have them baked into an oatmeal cookie. And to answer your question, I'm not hungry. Besides, we've got to get back on the trail."

"Wait just a minute!" Mr. Parker almost choked. He chewed furiously on a mouthful of the snack before resuming his rant. "This has become a forced march. I'm starving, and we haven't even had lunch yet. Tanner and I need some time to walk around and stretch before we get back on."

The muscles in Miya's shoulders tightened. She waited until she was sure her voice wouldn't shake. "You're right about lunch. I'll get everyone a sandwich to eat while we ride. Usually, we rest for a half hour, but we're running out of time." She pointed to the clouds gathering at the top of the ridge. "If we get going now, you'll be a little uncomfortable in the short run. If we wait around and it rains, you'll be miserable in wet sleeping bags tonight. Trust me, that's not very relaxing."

Mr. Parker glared at her but didn't reply.

Tanner looked from his dad to her. Finally, Mr. Parker nodded. "Okay."

Tanner opened his hand and dropped the raisins into the tall grass.

Miya helped Tanner up and handed him the reins. Instead of looking at her, Tanner gazed down at the spot where the raisins had disappeared.

"You should be nice, Miya," he said.

She stared at the little kid with thick glasses and an overly large T-shirt. Didn't he understand this was his dad's fault, not hers? She looked at the ground, regretting that last bit of sarcasm she used with Mr. Parker.

"You're right," she said. "I'll try to do better. Here's a sandwich. It's my specialty—peanut butter and strawberry jelly."

Miya gathered up her pack horses and got on Dream. From the corner of her eye, she watched Jake untie Crackerjack, check his cinch, and hand the reins to Mr. Parker.

"Before we go, I want to tell you about the creek we'll cross. It's more like a river. The bank is steep, so hold your horses back until the horse in front of you is at the water's edge." She pointed to Dream's lead rope tied in a half hitch around her saddle horn. "Loosen up your lead rope so the horse can drink. We'll wait in the middle until they're all finished. We'll ride single file to the other bank when they're all done. Ready?"

Tanner was the only one who responded. "What about Zoey?"

"Thanks for thinking of her. Zoey loves the water. She'll hop over these first rocks, jump into the middle, swim, and beat us to the other side. Anything else?"

Tanner spoke up again. "I'm a little scared."

"Oh, for Pete's sake." Mr. Parker gulped water from his Dior Aqua Bottle before saying, "Man up, Tanner."

Tanner's shoulders slumped.

Jake glared at the older man. "You don't have to be scared, Tanner. Dollar's crossed this creek a hundred times. Just give him his head, and he'll do the rest. When he starts walking across, watch the opposite shore instead of looking down at the water, and you'll be fine."

Miya flipped the lead rope over her head and transferred it to her right hand. "Hup, Daisy. Hup, Vista. Let's cross the creek."

"When they reached streamside, Dream eased into a deep cut in the bank. Thick brown roots covered with dirt and sand poked out of the side of the slope. The water splashed over the rocks, swirling into eddies and pools. A fish jumped, forming a single silver arc in the air before disappearing into the water below.

Miya leaned back, and Dream slid the last few feet, nearly sitting on her hind end. As Dream's shoes scraped against the rock, pebbles loosened and tumbled toward the creek. It had only been weeks since she had heard that same sound. The video replayed in her mind—the elk antler, brown against the patchy snow. Falling. Clawing the side of the mountain, terrified that her grip would loosen and that she'd plunge into nothingness.

Dream snorted and shook her head, ending Miya's misery. Miya took several deep breaths.

"Right, Dream, we need to move on." Miya asked the mare to take small steps to allow the pack horses time to drop off the bank safely. When they were all on level ground, Miya stopped Dream at the edge of the water and turned to watch Tanner.

"Miya, I can't do it!"

Miya looped the lead rope of the pack horses around her saddle horn in case she needed to bail off and help Tanner. "You can do it. Hold on tight to the horn. Trust Dollar."

"I can't." Tanner sounded as though he might burst into tears.

"I know how it feels to be scared, but you've got this. Dollar will take care of you."

Miya heard the scraping sound of sand and rocks above her. She strained to see through the brush. There was more shuffling. Within seconds, a small flurry of pebbles hit the bottom of the bank. Miya tensed, transferring her weight to the left stirrup to dismount.

As she swung her leg over the saddle, Dollar's head came into view. While chewing on a willow branch, he meandered to the end of the bank and hopped down. With a satisfied snort, Dollar trotted over to Dream.

Tanner's head snapped back when Dollar jumped. He was as pale as milkweed but was grinning by the time he reached Miya.

"You made it down the steep part! I knew you would." Miya reached over to give him a high five.

"Dollar and me did it together," Tanner said proudly. He petted the pony. "He's great, isn't he?"

Miya laughed at Dollar, who was chewing the last of the willow leaves. "You two make a good team."

After Mr. Parker and Jake joined them at the edge of the creek, Miya clucked to her horses, and Dream stepped into the water. She cautiously found her footing on the slippery round rocks of the riverbed. Miya looked back and saw Dollar step into the creek. The reins flapped as they worked their way up Dollar's neck. Tanner clutched the saddle horn with both hands.

Miya stopped Dream in the middle of the creek. The crashing sound of the water made it impossible for her to get Tanner's attention, but she needed to tell him to pick up his reins. When Dollar put his head down for a drink, the pony could step into the loop with his front feet. Miya imagined Dollar trying to lift his head, panicking, and throwing Tanner into the fast-moving water. At the very least, Tanner would get soaking wet. At the very worst, the current would carry him downstream, and he'd drown in this creek. It had happened to others. Why hadn't she reminded him to hold on to his reins with one hand and the horn with the other?

Miya stuck her saddle string in her mouth and bit down hard on the soft leather. It tasted of sweat and smelled like neatsfoot oil. It wasn't very tasty, but her fingernails were bloody and chewed down to the quick. As soon as Tanner got to the middle of the creek, she could maneuver her horses over and grab the reins before Dollar put his head down.

Turning in her saddle, Miya saw Crackerjack start into the water. Within minutes, Jake slid around Mr. Parker and urged Hawk into the creek. Dollar plodded across the water, testing each step before taking another. His nose skimmed the surface, reminding Miya of a large brown turtle.

Jake splashed through the water behind Tanner as Hawk and the pack horses left a wake of miniature white caps and bubbles. Jake rode alongside Tanner. "Pick up your reins."

Tanner looked at him in confusion. Jake held up his reins. "Get ahold of your reins before he puts his head down."

Tanner let go of the horn with his left hand and leaned forward. The loop of reins was directly behind Dollar's ears by now. Standing on tiptoes in the stirrups, Tanner managed to grab the reins and sit back in the saddle.

Jake smiled at Tanner, teeth flashing white against his tanned face. He pushed back his cowboy hat and tilted his head to catch the breeze. Miya caught Jake's eye, and she gave him a thumbs-up. Her heart beat a little faster as he nodded back at her.

"No!"

Startled, Miya swung around at the sound of Mr. Parker's cry.

"The Explorer!" Mr. Parker pointed to the water at Crackerjack's feet. "I dropped it!"

"Dream, you stay here." Miya knew it would take too long to get Dream and both pack horses to Mr. Parker. The Explorer would surely be washed away by then.

She jumped off the right side of her horse. The current was strong, and the rocks unstable beneath her feet. Miya grabbed the fender of her saddle and managed to stay upright. The bone-chilling, glacier-fed water swirled around her. Miya gasped. Letting go of the saddle, she took a tentative step toward Crackerjack. Her leather-soled boots were slippery as she slid over the algae-covered rocks.

"Whoa!" Miya held out her arms for balance. She inched forward, taking four more small steps. Just as she started to fall, Mr. Parker leaned over and grabbed her arm.

"Thanks." Miya had no control over her teeth chattering. "Whe... where did you drop it?"

Mr. Parker pointed at Crackerjack's front foot. Miya hung on to Mr. Parker's stirrup, waiting for the debris to settle.

"You didn't give us time to check the map when we stopped," Mr. Parker yelled over the sound of the water. "I wanted to see how much farther it was. When I took the Explorer out, this dumb horse started walking again."

Miya gripped the stirrup more tightly. She didn't understand why Mr. Parker called Crackerjack dumb when he was the one who took the Explorer out in the middle of a creek. Miya was about to mention this when she glanced at Tanner. He looked as though he were about to cry.

Miya hugged her arms closer to her body. "Good thing it's waterproof." She saw a flash of neon green on the bottom of the creek bed. Miya plunged her hand into the icy water and fished around until her fingers closed over the plastic case. "Got it!" She brought it to the surface with a sigh of relief. "Oh crap!" Miya said. She held up the Explorer.

"Either Crackerjack stepped on it, or it broke during the fall. See, the bottom part is missing, and the insides are ruined." Shivering, Miya handed the device to Mr. Parker. "Put what's left of it in your saddlebag." She turned to slide back to Dream, who had wandered a few feet away.

"This is unacceptable. As soon as I return, I'm contacting the company. That product is not as advertised. It fell apart—"

Miya took a careful step toward the horses.

"Miya, wait! I'm coming to get you." Jake rode toward Miya. She shielded her eyes with her forearm to avoid the worst of Hawk's splashes. Jake stopped beside her and leaned down. Miya stuck her foot in Jake's left stirrup and grasped his arm. She pushed against the slick rocks but lost her footing and could only lumber halfway on. Jake leaned away, pulling hard, and managed to haul her up and out of the creek. She landed with an ungraceful thump behind the saddle.

Miya rested her head against Jake's back, savoring his warmth and strength. After a minute, he spoke, "Why did you jump in the water after the Explorer? You have our Inreach, right?"

She shook her head. The worn fabric of Jake's shirt rubbed against her forehead. Aware that Mr. Parker was staring, Miya straightened. She didn't want him to think that Jake was in charge of this trip.

"No." Miya's face reddened with shame. "Since Mr. Parker had the newer, lighter model, I left yours in the truck. I should have brought both."

Jake was quiet for several seconds. Finally, he said, "No use crying over spilled milk, or in this case, creek water. I'll drop you off and get Dream and the other horses."

Miya watched Dream stand patiently in the middle of the creek. Vista, however, was pulling on her lead rope and pawing at the water. "Okay. We better hurry before Vista lies down and soaks her pack or trots away and heads back to the trailer."

"Follow us, guys," Jake shouted to Mr. Parker and Tanner as Hawk approached the opposite bank.

Jake dropped Miya off and handed her his pack horses. Miya led them up the trail until she found a log alongside it. She tied up the horses and eased down on the log to pull off her boots. Miya turned them upside down. Water spilled out. She peeled off her socks and wrung them out. Wet socks rubbing against wet ankles caused blisters in no time.

Miya tried to wring out the bottom of her jeans without much luck. She shivered. The sun was warm now, but sunset wasn't too far away. Then, the cold would settle in.

Zoey bounded up the trail. She whined and laid her head in Miya's lap. Miya hugged her. "Silly dog. You're almost as wet as I am."

Jake rode up, followed by Tanner and Mr. Parker. "Want me to find you some dry clothes?"

Miya shook her head. "No time. I don't even remember which horse has my duffel, so we might end up unpacking two or three. I'll change when we get to camp."

Jake frowned. "You sure? You'll be cold and miserable in about a half hour."

Setting her jaw, Miya said, "I'm sure." Her stomach started churning again. "I wish we hadn't lost the Explorer." She almost admitted how worried she was about it.

Tanner rode up beside her. "I'm sorry about the Explorer," he said. His voice cracked as he looked down at his saddle horn.

Miya pulled on her socks and tugged on her wet boots. She stood up and wiggled her cold toes. "No problem, Tanner." Miya bent the truth a little. "I've been on lots of pack trips and never had to use it. We probably won't have any emergencies on this trip either."

Shadows shifted as Miya stared into the timber. Hugging her arms tightly around herself, she shivered. *Why*, she wondered, *after I've planned so carefully, is disaster stalking me?*

Miya guided Dream into a small meadow beside the trail and motioned for the others to follow. She had ridden along for the last half hour, counting backward from one hundred to keep her mind off Wildcat Pass.

"This is a good place to get off and stretch and have another snack. Jake and I will tie up the horses."

Mr. Parker snorted. "I thought you were in a big hurry to get to camp." He gestured at the mountain with his chin.

"I am." Miya tied up Daisy. Her wet clothes clung to her, and she shivered, though only partly from the cold. "We're about to start up Wildcat Pass. We have to wait here and be sure no one else is coming over from the other side. The trail is too narrow to pass another pack string."

Tanner squinted down the path. "I can't see anyone coming. Tell me again. Why are we waiting?"

"The trail curves around the side of the mountain and disappears from our view," Miya said. "It does the same on the other side. If both groups wait a few minutes, they can see if another pack string has started around the curve."

"That sounds dangerous," Mr. Parker said. "I don't want Tanner or me to get hurt."

Jake spoke up. "All kinds of people ride over this trail to get to the high country. If we wait and watch, we'll be fine."

Tanner looked up at the mountain and swallowed hard. Miya put her arm around him. "Tanner, you're the safest of all of us since you're riding Dollar. He would never risk his chance for future cookies."

Tanner nodded without looking convinced.

"How about this?" Miya unbuckled her saddlebag. "I'll find my binoculars, and you can watch the trail for us."

Tanner held the binoculars up to his eyes, turning in a wide circle. Stopping, he focused on Miya. "Wow—your nose is ginormous!"

Miya punched him lightly on the arm. "You're supposed to be watching the trail, not my nose, thank you very much."

Jake gathered small twigs and arranged them in a circle of rocks beside the trail.

"What are you doing?" Miya asked. The words came out more sharply than she intended.

"Your lips are blue." Jake looked up from the dry pine needles he was busy scattering." If you warm up for twenty-five minutes by the fire, you'll feel better." Jake dug down into his chap pocket and pulled out a lighter.

Mr. Parker and Tanner overheard their conversation. She plastered a fake smile on her face. "There are apples and plums in Jake's saddlebag." She crouched down beside Jake. "Can we talk? Over there by Vista?"

Jake followed Miya to where the roan mare stood. "What's up?"

"We're not going to make a fire because we're not going to wait the whole thirty minutes. As soon as they finish their apples, we're going on."

Jake shook his head. "Dumb idea, Miya." You know it only works if both groups wait for half an hour on their side. It takes the full amount of time to see people coming around the turn."

Miya pointed at the sky. "We're hours behind. It's going to rain. By the time everyone gets back on their horses, fifteen minutes will have passed. That's enough."

Miya looked over Jake's shoulder. The mountain loomed tall and forbidding. She couldn't bear to tell him the other reason. If she didn't ride over that pass right now, the elephant sitting on her chest would suffocate her. She'd have to turn back, and they'd have to refund Mr. Parker's money, which they didn't have.

"It's my trip," Miya said. "I say we're going on. Chances are almost a hundred percent that we won't meet anyone coming out this late in the day."

"Fine. It's on you, Miya." Jake crossed his arms and glared at her. "Because…what if we do?"

Chapter Twelve

"Okay, guys, let's get back on our horses and across this pass." Miya's voice sounded high and shrill even to her ears. She watched Jake's jerky movements as he untied Crackerjack and handed Mr. Parker the lead rope.

"Can you do something about these stirrups?" Mr. Parker rubbed his leg. "My knees hurt."

Without a word, Jake slid the buckle down the stirrup leather. Grabbing the bottom of the stirrup, he jerked on it. *Crack*. The leather snapped into place. He did the same with the other stirrup.

"Problem solved. Your knees won't hurt, but your butt will."

Jake untied his pack horses and led them to Hawk. He threw himself into the saddle without bothering to put his foot in the stirrup. Frowning, Jake sat—jaw clenched, eyes staring straight ahead.

Miya leaned closer to whisper to Dream. "Jake thinks he knows everything." A headache pounded at the base of her skull. "We need to ride as far as possible while there's still daylight."

Miya inhaled, held her breath for a beat, and exhaled slowly. As soon as she put her foot into the stirrup, the world around her spun. Miya closed her eyes and held onto the front of her saddle. She was hot. Why was she so hot? She wiped the sweat off her forehead. When she opened her eyes, the mountain ahead was fuzzy around the edges.

"Miya, are you all right?" The worry in Tanner's voice caused her to look back.

She wanted to say she wasn't all right. She wanted to give in to the anxiety, turn around, and ride off this mountain. Instead, she took another deep breath. "I'm good. Follow me."

Although she shook so hard her teeth chattered, Miya mounted Dream. She nudged her with her heels. Dream's hooves scraped across rock as they started toward the trail. Miya stood in her stirrups and strained to see and hear what was ahead. It wasn't too late to turn back now, but they'd be committed in a matter of minutes.

Miya looked over her shoulder. Her pack horses fell into line behind Dream. Dollar ambled over to his place behind them, feet dragging, ears flopping back and forth like an old mule's.

Her heart slammed against her chest. It was beating its way upward, out of her throat. A heart attack! She was having a heart attack. Miya slid off Dream and closed her eyes. She leaned against her saddle for support.

She felt a hand on her shoulder and heard Jake's low, calm voice. The roaring in her ears was too loud for Miya to understand his words, but she recognized the steadiness in his tone. She turned and wrapped her arms around him. Jake rubbed her back and waited.

After a few minutes, Miya lifted her head off his shoulder. "Where are the others?"

"I sent them back to the meadow. I told them we were watching the trail a little longer."

"Do you think they suspect anything?"

"Nah. Well, Tanner, maybe. Parker's too into himself."

Taking a shaky breath, Miya asked, "What am I going to do?"

Jake scanned the low clouds before answering. "If you can't face the pass now, I have three ideas. One, we turn around and ride several hours back to the trailhead. You refund the money. Two, you go back, and I take them on into camp. Three, I lead everyone across. You follow at the end of the line, eyes closed if it helps, and trust Dream to get you there."

Miya glanced over her shoulder at the others. Mr. Parker was practicing some yoga poses.

Jake stirred. "Miya, it's getting late, and we're about to get soaked. Do you have any other ideas?"

She didn't. She couldn't leave Jake up here alone with these two and all the horses, and she most definitely wouldn't lead them all the miles back to the trailhead in disgrace. Mr. Parker would bask in her humiliation.

Miya climbed into the saddle. "The third choice. I'll do it."

Jake touched her knee. "Good for you. I'll call the others and start up the trail. Close your eyes or keep looking forward. Dream's got this. So do you."

Miya stuffed the end of the saddle string in her mouth and bit down hard. What if she got to the middle of the pass but couldn't continue on? It was too narrow for Dream to turn around. She'd be trapped.

As the other horses passed her, Tanner asked, "Why is Jake riding in the front?"

Miya slipped the saddle string out of her mouth and tried to keep her voice casual. "We decided to switch places for a while."

Mr. Parker muttered, "I don't care if you play musical chairs. Just get us to the damned camp."

Miya didn't have the strength to answer. She waited until Crackerjack was a horse's length ahead of her before she wrapped both hands around the saddle horn. "Step by step, Dream," she whispered, tapping the horse with her heels.

Clip, clop. Dream's hooves made a hollow sound in the dirt. Miya felt hyperaware of the sounds and the smells around her—especially the pungent tang of the manure on her boots. Zoey's wet dog scent lingered on Miya's damp clothes while her own sweat dripped off her nose. Miya couldn't let go of the saddle horn long enough to wipe it off.

"I am strong," Miya whispered. But a voice inside her head taunted her. *Liar! If you weren't petrified, you'd have this dumb anxiety under control, and you'd be up front where you belong instead of dragging behind eating dust.*

"Take action. Replace negative self-talk with positive." Miya said the words aloud. "That's what all the coaches on YouTube say."

Miya gripped the saddle more tightly with her legs. She wished she were back in her room, watching self-help videos on her phone.

Peering ahead, Miya noticed a stunted juniper growing from a crack in the rock on the side of the trail. "I can make it to that tree." While Dream's hooves clip-clopped down the trail, Miya concentrated on the fir-green color of the needles and how the trunk twisted toward the sunlight.

Her boot touched the juniper as she rode by. Miya rolled her shoulders while maintaining a death grip on the saddle horn. Dream drew to a halt, shaking her head.

"What is it, girl? Do you see something? Miya was afraid to twist in her saddle to check her backtrail in case she accidentally peeked over the edge. She leaned forward to see if another pack string was approaching. After determining the coast was clear, Miya craned her neck to scan the rock beside her. She'd heard that mountain lions sometimes waited on the ledges to ambush their prey.

Dream continued to stand rooted in one spot, shaking her head harder. What's wrong, girl?" Miya heard both the question and the sense of urgency in her voice. It was dangerous to stop a horse here. One misstep, and they'd fall off the trail. By pausing, she endangered not only her own life but three others.

Miya stared down at her hands. She realized she'd been holding onto Dream's reins too tightly, pulling back instead of allowing the mare to walk freely. Miya let the reins slide through her fingers. There was nothing wrong with the trail. Dream was reacting to Miya's panic.

"I'm okay. I can keep going." Miya focused on a curve in the path. She trusted Dream. She could make it around the next bend and the next until she topped over Wildcat Pass. She had no choice.

After Dream rounded the last curve, Miya slumped against the saddle. Her body felt as limp as a bowl of overcooked spaghetti. Staring across the landscape, Miya barely noticed the red Indian paintbrush and purple wildflowers dotting the hillside. Somehow, she'd done it. She'd made it over Wildcat Pass.

The eutrophic feeling was quickly replaced by embarrassment. She'd let her fears get the best of her—Jake had taken over. Miya felt her cheeks flame. This was her pack trip. She was supposed to be in control. Shaking off her exhaustion, Miya rode from the back of the group to join Jake at the front. Although Jake still sat easily in the saddle, Tanner and Mr. Parker looked somewhat worse for the wear. Tanner slumped forward against the seat, his shoulders hunched, his back rounded. Mr. Parker grimaced as he stood in his stirrups. After a few seconds, he sat down again, shifting his weight from side to side.

"See?" Miya pointed down the mountain. "Camp is just beyond that stand of pine trees. It's only a couple more miles. If you want, you can jump off and stretch again before we tackle the last part of the trail."

Miya knew she had talked too fast and too loudly, but the relief buzzing through her veins felt like she'd chugged three energy drinks in a row. She slid off Dream, her legs still trembling.

"I want down," Tanner said. He scrambled off Dollar.

Mr. Parker eased himself to the ground. "My backside will never be the same. Why didn't you tell me this trip was well over twenty miles?"

Confused, Miya repeated. "Twenty miles? It's only twelve. Fourteen by the time we get to camp."

Hands on his hips, Mr. Parker pivoted in a small circle. "Feels like twenty."

Miya laughed. "Only fourteen. I promise."

She looked down into a bowl where lodgepole pine grew. In the center was a meadow with a creek running alongside. Miya couldn't wait to set camp up—the horses munching on alfalfa cubes and the tents standing snug and warm. She pictured the curl of woodsmoke from the fire, and she could almost smell the aroma of coffee percolating.

Jake cleared his throat. "Miya!" He pointed to a wall of black clouds. "We need to get off this ridge!"

Miya realized that while she daydreamed, a storm was about to roll in. The air carried a chemical scent that was humid and heavy to breathe. Miya closed her eyes for an instant, remembering the backpacker who had been struck by lightning up here a year ago.

Moving quickly, Miya grabbed Dollar's lead rope for Tanner. When she touched the pony's neck, her fingers tingled with static electricity. "We'd better get going."

Tanner pulled up a clump of grass and offered it to Dollar. He wiped his hands on his jeans. "But I'm cold, Miya."

She shivered. "Me, too. I'll get your jacket."

Miya stood on Dream's lead rope and held onto Dollar with her left hand. Tanner's hoodie and one of Miya's old rain slickers were tied behind the saddle. She worked the knots of the saddle strings loose with her right hand and shook out Tanner's hoodie. "Here, put this on."

After some tugging, Tanner poked his head through the neck hole. The sweatshirt was well-worn and too small. His wrists protruded four inches from the cuffs.

"Your duffel is on a pack horse. You can put on your coat and some warmer clothes when we get to camp."

"But Miya, I don't..." Tanner's mouth quivered.

"My old slicker is too big for you, but it's better than nothing." Miya shifted from foot to foot. She needed this kid to hurry up. "We'll work it out when we get there."

Tanner sniffed. He stuck his arms into the sleeves. Miya hurriedly fastened the black snaps and boosted him up onto Dollar.

"Miya!" Tanner's hand had disappeared into the long sleeves of the slicker. "I have to tell you something."

Miya rolled up the left sleeve and handed Tanner the reins. "Tell me when we get to camp."

Crackerjack stood with his feet braced as Mr. Parker hauled himself into the saddle. Mr. Parker groaned. "What I wouldn't give for a hot tub and a massage right about now."

"How about a steaming cup of coffee and a warm sleeping bag?" Miya asked. She touched Dream with her heels, and the mare started down the hill at a fast walk.

The sky was an ominous charcoal gray, and the mist so thick it was almost rain. Moisture poured down Miya's cheeks like cold tears. She turned in her saddle. The horses had their ears pricked up, blowing small clouds of white smoke from their nostrils. They pulled at their reins and pranced, eager to get to camp.

Miya shouted above the gathering storm. "We can't let the horses go down this hill too fast. Ride single file behind me." She transferred her weight back in her saddle. "Slower, Dream. Let's get everyone to camp safely."

The trail bottlenecked at the drift fence. Miya looked at the three rails lying in the dirt. She needed to wait until Jake, who was last, got off and lifted the rails onto the crossbucks on either side of the trail. That way, if a horse got loose, it would be blocked from running away, maybe as far as the trailhead. Miya pulled on her reins.

Thunder crashed behind the bank of clouds, warning them that the storm was gathering force. It was only a matter of time before they were caught in a deluge.

Dream shook her head and barely slowed, unwilling to stop and wait at the drift fence. "You want to get to camp as much as I do." Dream shook her head again, harder and more impatiently. "All right, have it your way. We won't take the time to shut the gate now. I'll ride back tomorrow and set it up."

Chapter Thirteen

When they reached camp, Miya stopped Dream next to a dead tree. "Tie your horses over here." Miya had to raise her voice to be heard above the wind. She slid to the ground and crouched down to pet Zoey. She wished she could pull her bedroll off the pack horse, curl up in the bottom, and sleep for a week.

"Miya!" Jake yelled over his shoulder as he tied up Hawk. "The big tent is on Daisy."

Miya lifted her head. The wind blew fiercely around her, snatching at her cowboy hat. Miya could hear the storm's roar, building strength in the canyon above.

"Yes, and the smaller one is on Jubal," she called back.

Jake rummaged in his saddlebag for his headlamp. After switching it on, he moved to Daisy and began untying the box hitch that secured the load. Jake plunged his hand into the pannier.

"The hammer is in here." Hoisting the tent off the sawbucks, Jake balanced it on his shoulder. He looked over to where Miya still stood. "Miya, you good?"

Miya clenched her jaw to keep her teeth from chattering. She moved to find her headlamp. "Yep."

Mr. Parker appeared out of the darkness. "I came to organize things."

Miya opened her mouth to answer, to inform him that things were organized. Mr. Parker trotted up to Jake. Miya watched him go. She was too cold and exhausted to care.

Jake stopped for a second. "Do you know how to set up a tent?"

"I never have," Mr. Parker said. "Are there directions?"

Miya caught Jake's eye roll before he turned away. "No, we'll take care of it. After you put your slicker on, find Tanner and wait in that stand of trees. Later, you can drag bedrolls and duffels into this tent."

Miya felt a splat of rain. She fastened the top snap of her slicker to prevent the cold drizzle from sliding down her collar and soaking her shirt. Jake carried the tent to a square of level ground and dumped it in the dirt. Miya hurried to help unroll it. The two of them grasped opposite ends and stretched the tent out. It was heavy, slick, and wet.

Clank. Clank. Jake hammered the first stake into the ground.

After grabbing the tent poles, Miya attempted to fit two of the sections together. The wind drove the rain sideways in icy sheets. She felt for the threads on the end of the pole and tried to attach one end to the other. They didn't fit. Miya wondered if she had started the threads properly or if she were putting the wrong pieces together. She pulled the poles apart and tilted her neck to position the headlamp so she could see them better. It was a futile effort between the wind, rain, and mist.

Miya dropped the poles and blew on her numb fingers. She grabbed the other section of the pole and jammed the first one into it. Still, it didn't fit.

Seriously?" she screamed into the wind.

"Need help?" Jake asked. He had finished staking out the tent and was waiting for the poles.

Miya nodded. Jake felt around in his slicker pocket and pulled out a flashlight. He gave it to Miya. "Shine the light on the ends of the poles so I can see."

Miya turned on the flashlight. Jake looked at the poles, chose two, and quickly screwed them together. It took him only a few more minutes to assemble the others. Miya sighed with relief. She didn't have time to mess with poles. People needed shelter.

"How long do you think this rain will keep up?" Miya shivered.

A steady stream of water dripped off the brim of Jake's cowboy hat. By the light of her headlamp, Miya caught the flash of his smile. "Oh, you know how it is. Once the tent is set up, the rain quits." He glanced up at the sky. "But maybe that won't be true tonight."

Half an hour later, Miya pulled the saddle off Vista and plodded over to a fallen tree. She set the saddle in front of the others and tugged the end of a tarp over it. Her hands were freezing, so Miya took a minute to poke them between the snaps of her slicker and bury them in the front pocket of her hoodie.

Jake moved from horse to horse, pouring alfalfa cubes on the ground. The sound of horses crunching reminded Miya that it had been hours since she'd last eaten.

Footsteps approached. Mr. Parker materialized out of the mist. "I managed to set the Coleman stove up."

Miya tucked a pair of saddlebags under the tarp. She was so tired that even talking was an effort, but she managed to force out a single word. "Thanks."

"The starter button doesn't work."

Miya felt like pounding her head against a ponderosa pine. After the first week, the starter button on Coleman stoves never worked. She wondered if the man had ever been camping before. Had he even heard of matches?

"I found the kitchen matches and lit it. I poured the chili out of the plastic bag into a pot. Tanner is watching it now."

"Great." Miya hoped Mr. Parker remembered to return the matches to the waterproof bag.

"The thing is, Tanner and I are cold."

Miya wanted to tell him to cowboy up. She was cold, too, but she swallowed her words. "There are two lanterns in red plastic cases. If you light them both, the tent will warm up quickly."

Mr. Parker flapped his arms. Startled, Vista jumped sideways. She nearly landed on Miya's toe, but Miya jerked her foot back in the nick of time.

"I don't know anything about lanterns!" Mr. Parker's voice rose as though he were about to have a temper tantrum.

"Got it," Miya said. "One of us will be there in a minute."

With a rustle of his slicker, Mr. Parker turned toward the tent. "Hurry, please."

As soon as Mr. Parker was out of earshot, Miya heard Jake snorting with laughter.

"If you think he's so funny, why don't you light the lanterns?"

"No way. I've got to put the food in the cache," Jake said. Miya heard the pulleys clink as he untangled the rope.

"Rock, paper, scissors?" she asked.

Jake laughed harder. "Nope. Your trip. Your responsibility. Remember?"

Miya wished she'd never uttered that now infamous line. "I'm going, and after we eat, I'll set up the other tent."

Jake attached the pulley to one of the panniers containing food for the rest of the trip. "You don't need to do that. Mom's not going to make it in tonight."

"Yes, she is. She'll ride in any minute now."

The rain let up, but water still dripped steadily from the tree branches. A sliver of moon sat high on the top of the ridge.

"Don't think so." Jake stared up the trail as though willing Janelle to appear. "She should have been here hours ago."

Miya didn't want to admit it, but Jake was right. "Maybe she waited out the rain, or maybe it took your dad longer to drive to the vet." Miya picked up the hammer. "The other tent will be too crowded with everyone's boots and all their stuff, so I'll set up a girls' tent."

Her voice faded. A picture of Jake's mom lying unconscious in a boulder field at the bottom of the mountain flashed through her mind.

"Okay, fine," Jake said. "If it makes you feel better, set up the tent. Just trying to save you some work."

Miya dropped the hammer and hugged Jake. The slicker made it feel like she had her arms around a giant roll of plastic. "I'm worried about your mom, too. Should we go look for her?"

"No." Jake didn't hug her back. "Too dangerous in the dark. I'll wait till morning."

Miya motioned toward the big tent. "I'll light the lanterns and check on supper."

Jake nodded as he hauled the first pannier up the tree.

Miya's slicker flapped around her legs as she approached the big tent. A flashlight beam bounced along the walls. Miya heard Tanner's high-pitched voice and the murmur of Mr. Parker's lower one. As she moved closer, she picked up the words of their conversation.

"Here's another flashlight, Dad. You can keep it. I have more of them in my duffel." Almost instantly, Miya watched a second beam play across the canvas. "Can you make the lantern work, Dad? I can help. I'm good at solving puzzles. Maybe we can find a switch or something."

"I don't see a switch or how it works. We'll have to wait. One of our guides will be here soon."

"Guides?" Tanner asked. "You mean Miya and Jake? I like them, don't you, Dad? They're nice, and they know about outdoor stuff I don't know about. You understand outside things cuz you go fly fishing and skiing. Have you camped out overnight a bunch?"

To her surprise, Miya heard a low rumble of laughter. "I do know quite a bit about the outdoors, but I haven't camped out much. The last time I slept in a tent, I was in my friend Byron's backyard. I was about your age. We spent all afternoon preparing the 'campsite' with cans of SpaghettiOs, sleeping bags, and our Game Boys. After slurping SpaghettiOs topped with Beanie Weenies, we crawled into our sleeping bags. It was Byron's idea to have a contest of who could tell the scariest story. Although I never admitted it, Byron knew I was petrified of mummies and rats. He told a story about a mummy that exploded, and hundreds of rats swarmed out of its belly to attack a kid camping in his friend's backyard."

"That's disgusting," Tanner said, "and scary."

Miya ducked through the tent flap. Both father and son had their backs to her, so she waited to hear the end of Mr. Parker's tale. "When we finally said goodnight, a mosquito buzzed around my ear, so I scooted to the bottom of my sleeping bag. It was stuffy down there, but even worse, all I could see was the mummy's grinning skull and hear its clacking teeth. I hightailed it to Byron's house, where I spent the rest of the night in the bathroom. Let this be a lesson to you. Never mix Beenie Weenies and SpaghettiOs."

Although Miya smiled, she hoped the story wouldn't give Tanner nightmares tonight. Suddenly, she noticed a burning smell. Miya turned toward the Coleman stove in time to see the chili overflow the pot and sizzle in the flame below.

"Oh, no!" Miya grabbed a potholder from the top of the kitchen pannier and shoved the pot onto the second unlit burner.

*Sizzle...sizzle...*the flame died with a *pff.*

Halfheartedly, Miya waved the potholder at the smoke.

At that moment, Jake entered the tent—taking in the three shocked faces and the pool of chili overflowing the pot.

"I like my chili hot, but you guys are taking it to extremes." He picked up a spoon and stirred the chili. "Can we salvage any of it?" he asked Miya. "Or is it a peanut butter and jelly night?"

Miya's laughter emerged in an unladylike snort. "Today hasn't been our day, but tomorrow's got to be better. Right?" She held out her hand for the spoon. "If you show these guys how to light the lanterns, I'll separate the good part from the scorched and add more tomato sauce. I'm so hungry, I'd eat it—burned bits and all."

Chapter Fourteen

Miya sat bolt upright, heart racing. Hoofbeats hammered against the ground. Horses nickered shrilly back and forth to each other. Surrounded by thick darkness, Miya reached for the bedside lamp, but it wasn't there. Instead, her fingers brushed the stiff canvas of her bedroll. With a jolt, Miya remembered. The pack trip! The pass! Lying awake for hours, worrying about Janelle! Miya fumbled under her pillow for a flashlight.

Zoey stood in the doorway of the tent barking furiously. Miya slipped out of her sleeping bag, pulled on her boots, and rushed outside.

"Hush, Zoey." Zoey quieted but continued to growl deep in her throat. Her ears were flattened against her head.

Jake hurried from his tent. The beam of his headlamp bobbed along the trees. "Miya, you okay?"

"Yeah, but Zoey's upset."

"So are the horses."

Miya looked out in the field. Dawn had colored the dark sky a watery shade of pink and orange. As the sun ascended, one thing was clear—the horses were gone. All of them. Even Dream. In the distance, Miya heard a branch crack as they galloped toward the trailhead.

A thick layer of frost coated the ground. Miya pulled her hands into the sleeves of her sweatshirt and flipped up her hood. "Why did they leave camp?" Each word dissolved into a tiny puff of whiteness.

The grass crunched as Jake studied the ground underneath the tree, where most of the food was stored on a wooden platform in the branches. He shone a flashlight at the bottom of the tree. "A bear. Look. There's a bunch of tracks here."

As she headed toward Jake, Miya noticed a metal object glinting in the brush—one aluminum side of a bear-proof pannier that had been stored at the bottom of the tree. The bear must have dragged it away and abandoned it when he couldn't open it. Miya traced her fingers over the claw marks and dents.

"Are you crying?"

"No! I'm trying to figure out how to get the horses back."

Jake threw an arm around her shoulder and touched her forehead with his. "I have a plan. After breakfast, we'll head down the trail about a mile and a half to the drift fence and catch them. After that, I'll ride out and meet Mom."

The excited voice of Tanner carried across the camp. Miya couldn't make out all the words, but she did hear the name "Dollar" quite a few times.

She pulled away and faced Jake. "Remember? We didn't shut the drift fence."

Jake smiled. "*You* didn't shut it. You were so focused on getting to camp you never looked back when I jumped off and got it."

Relief swelled in Miya's chest. "Really? You closed it? Why didn't I hear the horses going crazy?"

Miya knew it would have taken Jake at least ten minutes to drag the rails across the trail and position them. She pictured the pack horses nickering and running back and forth, worried that the rest of the group had left them behind.

Jake tugged lightly on her braid. "The wind was too loud."

Miya closed her eyes and leaned into Jake. "Thank you."

He held her for another minute as the sun struggled to rise above the mountain. "Like I said before we left, you don't have to keep trying to do this alone."

Miya nodded against his shoulder. "I know. I think I'm trying to prove to myself that I'm okay, that I can handle stuff, even with this anxiety."

Jake shook his head. "You don't need to prove anything."

Miya blew out her breath and attempted to explain. "This anxiety stuff. It's like being alone in a black room, and the door slams shut." Miya traced the scar along the length of Jake's index finger. "What would you do?"

Jake smiled. "That's easy. I'd find a window." He squeezed her hand. "Then, I'd text my friend for help."

The warmth of the red-yellow flames heated Miya's cheeks as she checked the pan of boiling water on the fire. Tiny bubbles had formed around the sides. Instant oatmeal was only minutes away.

"Bacon almost ready?"

From behind the Coleman stove, Jake saluted her with a fork. "Working on my last batch."

Wrapping her hands around her mug, Miya sipped cowboy coffee. The three heaping teaspoons of sugar she had stirred in masked its bitterness.

From somewhere high above the ridge, a rock slid down the mountain. It crashed and bounced—the sound muted by distance. There was silence for a minute. Another rumble followed.

"What's that?" Tanner's voice came from across the fire. He wore the same hoodie as yesterday and huddled as close to the blaze as he could get. Tanner's boots were nearly in the flames. Smoke billowed around him, yet he made no move to shift positions.

"Rocks rolling down the mountain. Happens all the time." Miya pointed to some boulders in the meadow. "That's how those got there."

"Oh." Tanner's eyes flicked over the rocks and back to the fire.

"Better move your boots back before they get burned."

"My feet are cold." Tanner coughed.

Miya took off her jacket. "Looks like you're cold all over. Here. Why don't you wear my coat for now. What happened to yours?"

Tanner pulled his foot back from the fire and stamped it. "That's what I tried to tell you yesterday. I didn't bring one."

Miya raised her eyebrows. "Okay, no coat. We can figure it out. Your dad packed everything else on the list, right?"

"What list?" Tanner stuck his arm into the sleeve of Miya's coat. "I packed myself." He looked at the ground. "And I might have forgotten my inhalers."

Jake arranged the last of the bacon on the plate. "Why do you need inhalers?"

"Asthma." Tanner zipped the jacket. "It's pretty bad." He coughed again. The cough rattled deep in his chest.

Her mouth suddenly dry, Miya swallowed hard to get some spit going. Mr. Parker had never said one word about asthma and inhalers. Miya's friend Lily had asthma. Lily didn't ride too much in the high country because the thin air made it hard for her to breathe.

"Come here." Miya pulled Tanner to his feet. "Sit over here, out of the smoke."

Tanner allowed himself to be led to a frayed red camp chair. He threw himself into it and wiped his nose on Miya's jacket sleeve.

Miya gulped her lukewarm coffee. She choked on the grounds and spat them out.

"It's probably just a misunderstanding. I'll talk to your dad, and everything will be cleared up."

Tanner puffed out his lips. "*Pff.* Good luck getting him to listen to you."

Miya pointed to the packets of instant oatmeal and the box of powdered sugar doughnuts. "You guys go ahead and eat breakfast. I'll see if your dad has your inhalers."

Tanner shook his head.

Closer to the creek, the heavy carpet of pine needles smelled of dampness and decay. Miya stamped through them, leaving a path of dark footprints in the wake.

Miya raised her voice. "Mr. Parker!"

The tent flap rustled, and Mr. Parker emerged. He wore a beige fishing vest and carried his fly rod in a case. His ball cap read SAGE CREEK FLY FISHING.

"I know you've got to round up the horses, but Jake can still take Tanner and me fishing. Right?" Mr. Parker asked. "I'd like to get an early start."

Miya's mouth fell open. "Uh…" She stumbled over the angry words vying to escape from her mouth. "The horses." Miya shook her head. "Tanner's coat." Finally, she managed to string together a full sentence, although its content surprised her. "The fish are still asleep."

Mr. Parker chuckled. Miya didn't bother to explain she wasn't being funny. *I thought all fly fishermen knew that insects don't like cold water.*

Taking a deep breath, Miya waved her hands in front of her. "That's not important now. Do you have Tanner's inhalers?"

Mr. Parker took off his ball cap and scratched his head. "No-o." He drew the word out. "Tanner has them. I asked him twice if he'd packed them. He promised me he had."

Miya's heart kicked in her chest. "He doesn't. Let's look in his duffel. Maybe we'll find them."

Mr. Parker entered the tent with Miya close on his heels. He unzipped Tanner's duffel and emptied the contents onto his sleeping bag. Kneeling beside it, Miya scanned the items in the dim light of the tent door. Underwear, several pairs. An assortment of socks, mostly with holes. Three short-sleeved T-shirts, one read EAT, SLEEP, GAME in glow-in-the-dark letters. A notebook, a pen, two flashlights, and a small stuffed fox, one eye missing.

Miya rubbed her forehead, noting all the things that weren't there. No warm coat, hat, or gloves. No long-sleeved shirts, long johns, or Chapstick. Worst of all, no inhalers. Miya picked up the duffel and ran her hands along the mesh pockets on the outside. Nothing. As her shoulders drooped with disappointment, Miya stuffed her hand into the cellphone pocket one more time. Her fingers touched something cold and metallic.

Grinning with relief, Miya closed her fingers around the object. Tanner had packed his inhaler, after all. He'd just forgotten what pocket he put it in. Miya pulled the tube from the pocket. Her smile faded when she realized it wasn't the inhaler. It was another flashlight, bright orange this time.

With a sigh, Miya climbed to her feet and pushed back the tent flap. "Let's talk to Tanner. After that, we'll figure out what to do next."

When Mr. Parker and Miya left the tent, Miya noticed Tanner's chair had shifted farther from the flames. Now, no matter which direction the wind blew, Tanner was clear of the smoke. To compensate for the lost warmth, Jake's coat draped across Tanner's lap.

Miya studied the nine-year-old. Tanner's cheeks were pink, and she thought his eyes looked brighter. His foot, clad in a dingy sock, was crossed over his knee. Jake stood beside him, wrapping duct tape around the sole of Tanner's boot.

Mr. Parker looked from Jake to Tanner. "What happened?'

Tanner shrugged. Jake tore the duct tape off the roll and smoothed down the end. "Just a little problem with boots and fire. This ought to take care of it." Jake handed Tanner the boot,

"Oh geez. Now it's the boots." Mr. Parker said.

A fat tear flowed from Tanner's eye and dripped onto the silver duct tape.

Hopping up and down on one foot, Miya pulled off her boot and handed it to Jake. "Wrap a little bit of that around the hole in my boot, would you?" She glared at Mr. Parker. "At one time or another, we all have to use duct tape to patch up our boots. Right, Jake?'"

Jake tore off a strip and smoothed it down. "Right." He winked at Tanner. "You're one of us now."

Mr. Parker marched over to Tanner and looked down at his son. "You promised me that you packed your inhalers and... Where's your coat?"

Tanner picked at the duct tape. "I did pack my inhalers, but I got them out to use one more time and forgot to put them back. Sorry, Dad." Tanner set his donut on the ground.

Mr. Parker sighed loudly. "That's just great. And your coat?"

Tanner dropped the boot and tugged it on. "It's summer! You never told me I needed a coat!"

"I didn't think I had to explain every little detail! This is a pack trip in the mountains!"

"I'm just a kid." Tanner's eyes welled with unshed tears. "It's not fair that I have to remember everything!"

Miya cleared her throat. "Let's think about how we're going to fix this. Tanner, how do you feel right now?"

"Fine." He spit the word out.

"First things first," Miya said. "We need to catch the horses. Hopefully, they're hanging out at the drift fence. Jake and I will go find them while you stay here with your dad and rest."

Mr. Parker reached for a donut. "Tanner says he's fine." After taking a big bite, Mr. Parker chewed quickly and swallowed. He reached for a paper towel and dabbed his lips. "How about this? Miya and Tanner catch the horses. While they're gone, Jake and I fish."

Miya bit the inside of her bottom lip. Mr. Parker seemed as clueless as a brand-new sixth grader on the first day of middle school. Why couldn't he understand that catching a few trout wasn't a priority to anyone except him?

Calm. She struggled to find calm. Miya wondered if the life coaches who gave advice on YouTube ever had to deal with a Mr. Parker.

Miya considered the situation. First, she thought about the horses. They didn't need two people to catch them. Zoey and one person could bring the horses back to camp. Plus, if the group had to pull out early because of Tanner's asthma, Mr. Parker needed an opportunity to fish. He might not sue, but he seemed like the type of person to post a nasty review or want his money back if he didn't get what he'd paid for. Miya pictured the budget notebook. That money turned some of the red numbers black.

Jake sat in a camp chair, tapping his foot on the ground. Miya knew he was itching to grab his binoculars and jog down the trail to see if he could spot his mom.

"This is what we're going to do. Jake and Zoey will gather the horses. Mr. Parker, Tanner, and I will fish some of the creeks around here."

Mr. Parker opened his mouth, but Tanner spoke up first. "I'm going with Jake."

Miya shook her head. "It's pretty far to the drift fence. The more you move around, the harder it will be to breathe."

Tanner looked at Jake, his eyes pleading. "Tell them I'm going with you, Jake."

Jake stood up and touched Tanner's shoulder. "It should be okay. It's an easy downhill trail to the fence, and we'll take it slow. I'll put Tanner on Dollar and lead him back if necessary." Jake turned to Miya. "Sound good, boss? See you about 1:00?"

Miya smiled at him. She knew the word "boss" had been for Mr. Parker's benefit.

"That work for you, Mr. Parker?"

Mr. Parker finished his donut and reached for another. "I suppose it will have to. One more thing. How dangerous are these bears and why wasn't I informed about them?"

"You were informed." Miya mentally rolled her eyes. "The bear country information was part of the attachment my dad sent you. It was right after the list of things to pack. You signed off on it when you came out to the ranch."

Mr. Parker frowned. "I might have skipped the part about bears."

Behind Mr. Parker's back, Jake winked at Miya. "Bears can be dangerous, but we've never had too much of a problem with them. We follow the Forest Service guidelines, like keeping a clean camp, carrying bear spray, and staying aware. Last night's bear was probably hoping for a handout and spooked the horses on his way to the creek when he couldn't find any food."

"I have bear spray," Mr. Parker announced.

"Good," Miya said. "Keep it handy."

Chapter Fifteen

Hands on her hips, Miya turned slowly, surveying the camp. The cook tent stood at the edge of the clearing. The two sleeping tents crouched about forty feet away. The breeze snapped the canvas door of the closest tent. Miya stooped to make sure the snaps were all fastened tightly.

She'd worked for an hour securing the area in case the bear decided to visit again. The food was back up in the tree, and the camp chairs and other gear were stowed in the tents. The bear-proof panniers contained one bag of horse feed and all the dog food. Miya poked in the fire pit with a stick. The last of the charred wood sat in a gray puddle of water. Since the bear hadn't been rewarded with any food last night, she hoped he would move on to better pickings.

Sitting down on a stump, Miya pulled on her waders. Her tippet, forceps, and nippers dangled from the lanyard around her neck, gently bumping against her chest. She assumed Mr. Parker had his own, much better, expensive tools, but she no longer cared how Mr. Parker viewed her. She was the guide, and she was good at it.

Miya picked up her net. "Mr. Parker, are you ready?"

Mr. Parker ducked out of his tent, carrying a custom-made bamboo fly rod. "Lead on."

The first fishing spot was half a mile from camp. Careful to keep their shadows off the water, they stopped near a pool on the creek. Miya noticed a hatch of mayflies rising off the slow water near the bank. Their delicate blue wings looked like fairy wings. Mayflies flew up into the sunlight and flared out like sparklers on the Fourth of July.

Miya crouched next to the shore. She turned a rock over and pointed to the round caddis pupae clinging to its underside like tiny, purplish brown beads. Mr. Parker nodded. "That helps me decide what to start with. He turned away, opening his box of flies. Miya didn't hear what combination he had chosen.

She shrugged. Most clients asked for advice, but it was clear Mr. Parker didn't need her opinion. It looked like her role today consisted of wading into the water and freeing the line from snags. Miya wished she was the one fishing. Knee-deep in the sparkling water. Back casting, pausing, and accelerating to a front cast. As she laid her line out straight over dark water, the soothing rhythm would ease her worries about Jake's mom, Tanner's asthma, and the missing horses.

Instead, Miya waited, ready to free a line or scoop a trout into her net. She passed the time by chewing on blades of grass and thinking about Jake. He was one of the most popular kids in school. Athletes were always popular, but beyond his jock status, Jake took the time to see people honestly. He said hi to everyone. It didn't matter if they were a nerd, a band geek, or a gamer. Jake even greeted the kids who hid in the shadows.

Miya wished she could be more outgoing at school, but she always worried that kids wouldn't say hi back to her when she passed them, so the words piled up and stuck in her throat until the opportunity passed.

Miya sighed. She might be shy, but at least she wasn't as obnoxious as Aurora and Brinley. To take her mind off those two, Miya admired Mr. Parker's fly rod. She'd never seen one as beautiful with its dark caramel color and jewel-like hardware. If Miya ever won the lottery, she'd order a rod just like that from the best custom designer in the West.

She and Mr. Parker gradually worked their way upstream. He caught a couple of nice browns, which they admired, snapped pictures of, and released back into the pools of shadow and stones.

The sun wasn't quite overhead when Mr. Parker suggested they take a break. He and Miya climbed up the bank and into the coolness of the forest. A pine squirrel dashed along a low limb, flipping his tail as he disappeared. Miya and Mr. Parker sat on a downed tree. He pulled a package of beef jerky from his pack and offered it to Miya.

She read the label. "Mango Habañero. Jerky?"

"Best jerky you'll ever eat. Mr. Parker opened his pocketknife and cut off the top of the package. "Handcrafted. If you prefer, I have some Teriyaki Orange."

"This is fine." Miya wondered when companies started pairing fruit and jerky. She took a tentative bite. Unlike the jerky her mom bought, this melted in her mouth. It tasted weird, but it was tender.

"Like it?" Mr. Parker asked.

Miya took another bite. "I think so." She watched a red ant travel the length of the limb beside her. He carried a twig in his mouth almost as long as he was.

"You going to be a sophomore next year?"

Miya swallowed her jerky. "Junior." She looked at her waders, hoping she didn't have to try and make awkward conversation with Mr. Parker. She sipped her water.

"What's your favorite subject? Math?"

Miya sighed. She hated the What's-your-favorite-subject? question grownups always asked. Still, she had to give him points for trying to talk to her. "No, I'm not a big fan of math. I like art."

She waited for Mr. Parker to snicker and say something condescending—like math would take her farther in the world than art—but he only nodded and stared out toward the water.

Miya finished her jerky and pulled two apples from her pockets. She held one out to Mr. Parker, who shook his head.

Twirling the apple stem between two fingers, Miya thought about Tanner. He was smart and funny, yet his dad showed little interest. For Tanner's sake, Miya should say something. But would Mr. Parker listen to her? He seemed the kind of person who only listened to important people. He wouldn't bother with a teenage girl, especially a plus-sized girl with a pimple on her chin. She should let it go. It wasn't her business.

Yet, like a terrible playlist looping in her mind, Miya heard the pain in Tanner's voice after his dad yelled at him this morning. The least Miya could do was talk to him. She opened her mouth, but the words congealed into a hard lump in her throat. She cleared it. With an effort, she managed to blurt out, "Tanner's a good kid."

Hidden behind expensive polarized sunglasses, Mr. Parker's eyes were unreadable. He was quiet for several seconds before saying, "If you say so."

Miya's eyes widened. "Why do you say that?"

Mr. Parker opened the second package of jerky. He clicked his pocketknife closed. "I don't know him. I only get to see him for two weeks in the summer. Last August, we went to an amusement park. He threw up corn dogs and grape slushie all over his shirt and my shoes."

"You talk to him during the year, right?"

"Tanner gets on his phone, and we Facetime once a month. Funny how the timing of the conversation usually coincides with the date my child support is due."

A heaviness settled in Miya's heart. She was mostly sad for Tanner but a little bit for Mr. Parker. A fly buzzed around her apple. She swatted it. "It's not too late, you know."

"Isn't it?" The words were clipped. Bitter.

Miya stood up. "He's nine. Nine-year-olds still love their dads. You have to figure out how to show him you love him." Miya hesitated, gathering her courage. "You can start by listening to him."

"I do listen." Mr. Parker jammed the jerky into his pack. "When he has something worthwhile to say."

"Okay, fine." Miya shrugged and picked up the net.

"What is 'Okay, fine' supposed to mean in that tone?"

Miya squeezed the handle of the fishing net. "It means that it's not worth my time arguing with you because you're not willing to listen. I've only known Tanner a couple of days, but already I can see he has lots of worthwhile things to say." Miya picked up her pack. "Why don't you try to see things from his point of view?"

Cheeks burning, Miya wondered where those words had come from. She typically clammed up when there was any potential for conflict, especially with a client. And Mr. Parker was a client. An obnoxious, arrogant client. *Her* client.

Mr. Parker stared at her, open-mouthed, but his reaction and her words suddenly no longer mattered. Footsteps. They heard footsteps. Running footsteps.

"Miya!" Jake yelled. "Where are you?"

"Here! On the bank."

Miya heard Jake crash through the underbrush. He stopped in front of them, chest heaving, sweat matting the hair on his forehead.

Miya dropped her pack. Her heart pounded. "What's the matter?"

"I've got to go find Mom." Jake bent over, put his hands on his knees, and sucked in gulps of air.

Miya moved closer and laid a hand on his back. "What do you mean, find your mom?"

Jake stood up, still breathing hard. "Tanner and I caught the horses. I looked down the trail, hoping to see her."

Miya nodded. "And?"

Jake shook his head. "There's a rockslide. A big one. Took out the whole trail."

The blood pounded in Miya's ears. Lightheaded, she sank onto the downed tree. "Do you think your mom was caught in it?"

"Maybe. I don't know."

Miya had watched a rockslide a few years ago. It happened two ridges over from where she had been riding. She heard a roaring sound above her. The ground shook as rocks rolled down the side of the mountain. Within minutes, the slide had gathered enough momentum to push truckloads of sand, boulders, and entire trees into the bottomless canyon below.

If Janelle had been riding up the trail when an avalanche started, there was no way she could have escaped. Miya groaned softly to herself. She pictured Janelle at the kitchen table, her hand covering Miya's. Miya recalled the smile in Janelle's voice when she had offered to ride along on this trip. Now, Janelle could be hurt or even dead—all because Miya had to prove she could handle her anxiety.

Mr. Parker stepped up beside Miya. "Odds are she wasn't caught in it."

Jake glared at him. "There's still a chance. I've got to check it out."

Mr. Parker looked around. "Where's Tanner?"

Jake glanced over his shoulder. "Back at camp with Zoey."

"You left him? What if a bear attacks him?"

Jake turned to Mr. Parker. "A bear can't wander into camp and grab a kid in broad daylight in the ten minutes it took me to find you."

"Besides," Miya jumped to her feet, "if a bear happened by, Zoey would chase him off." She gave Jake a quick hug. "Go on. Be careful. We'll handle stuff here."

Casting a doubtful glance at Mr. Parker, Jake nodded and sprinted toward the trail.

When Miya and Mr. Parker returned to camp, Tanner sat on the ground beside Zoey. He was busy whittling a small tree limb with a cheap pocketknife.

Miya sat cross-legged on the ground beside them. "Whatcha doing?"

"Jake said I could use my new knife to make marshmallow roasting sticks." Tanner pared off a few more chips of wood. "Is Jake okay?"

"Yep, he's fine." As she told the white lie, Miya mentally crossed her fingers. She hoped Jake was fine. She pictured him climbing dangerously unstable rocks and calling out for his mom.

"Stop it, Miya," she whispered the words to herself. She couldn't let her imagination run away—Mr. Parker and Tanner depended on her. Eager to keep her anxiety in check, Miya turned her attention toward the meadow—naming each horse as she counted them in the field. Dream, Hawk, Dollar, Vista, Crackerjack, Jubal, Daisy, and the other pack horses—all grazing peacefully.

"Looks like you found all the horses," Miya said.

Tanner leaned the marshmallow stick against a stump, grabbed another one, and shaved the end into a point. "You should have seen Zoey." His voice rose with excitement. "The horses all spread out in the field, except for Dollar and Vista. Those two pushed against the fence with their chests."

"That pair doesn't give up easily." Miya checked the field again to make sure Dollar and Vista were still in camp.

Tanner nodded. "Zoey crouched down, but after Jake said 'Go by' and pointed, Zoey ran around and gathered all the horses into a group."

Mr. Parker sat down in a camp chair. He leaned forward, elbows on his knees.

"It's cool to watch a cow dog work, isn't it?" Miya reached out and scratched Zoey's head.

Tanner nodded and continued his story. "And when Jake said 'Look back,' Zoey ran out to round up Dollar and Vista. Then, Jake boosted me up on Dollar, and we hurried superfast back to camp.

He didn't joke around like he always does. I think he's worried about something."

Miya kissed Zoey on the tip of her cold nose. "Nice work." She scrambled to her feet. "Jake's checking something out, but it'll be fine."

Miya reached into the kitchen pannier and found the hand sanitizer. Squirting the gel on her palms, she rubbed her hands together until it evaporated. "It's time for lunch. You and your dad take charge of the pork and beans while I cook the burgers."

Tanner looked hopefully at Mr. Parker. "Want to, Dad?"

"I don't know how," Mr. Parker said.

"Nothing to it," Miya interrupted. "You two can throw in some ketchup, brown sugar, a splash of mustard. Whatever tastes good."

Mr. Parker sighed as he stood up. "Let me put this rod away, and we'll give it a try."

Miya dried her hands and hurried to meet him. After she hugged Jake tightly, she pulled away.

"Any sign of your mom?"

"No, there wasn't."

Miya studied him carefully. Jake wore his "I'll-make-it-through-this" face. It was the same mask he hid behind in the ER after a bull had hooked him.

She closed her eyes and covered them with her hands. "Oh, Jake." She stopped, unable to say more. The idea of Janelle caught in the rockslide was just too awful to think about.

After a few seconds, Jake swallowed hard. "I'm going to tell you the truth, Miya, but I want you to promise you won't freak out."

Head pounding, Miya whispered, "Freak out?"

Jake raised his eyebrows. "Yes, freak out. I know you, Miya."

Miya sighed. "Just tell me."

"The rockslide's a big one." Jake took out his phone. "You can't see it too well here, but it doesn't cover the trail for just a few feet or even a few blocks. I spent all day trying to find a way out. There's no way to get us or the horses over the slide. It's blocked the trail for miles."

Grabbing the phone, Miya held it closer. "No, it can't be. There's got to be a way around it!"

"You said you wouldn't freak out." Jake rubbed the back of his neck. "There's nothing much we can do about it. I keep telling myself that Mom's safe. That she got as far as the slide, turned back, and called the Forest Service. They'll try to blast and shovel us out."

Miya looked from Jake to the phone. She spoke out loud, "It could take weeks." Inside, she thought… *if your mom even made it out.*

Bewildered, Miya gazed at the phone for a few more seconds. She handed it back to Jake and turned to stare down the trail. "Do you think your mom is okay?"

Jake nodded. "I hope so. I keep adding up the time in my mind. Two hours to drive home from the trailhead, an hour at the vet, an hour to get home. Catching another horse, driving back, packing up. The rain probably slowed her down even more. I don't think she could have topped Wildcat Pass by the time the avalanche occurred."

Miya hugged herself tightly. Deep down, she didn't know if Jake truly believed his timeline, but for the sake of her sanity, she held on to it. They still had the problem of Tanner, though. No one realized they had a sick kid in camp.

"I'm riding down there. Maybe I can find a way out that you missed." Miya rubbed her arms. "We can't be trapped."

Jake held out his binoculars. "Take these. You're wasting your time. Looks like we're going to be here a while."

Miya jogged out to the meadow and jumped up on Dream. She trotted down the trail with Zoey at the mare's heels.

When they got to the edge of the field, Miya stopped Dream and stared in disbelief. Jake hadn't exaggerated. Stretching as tall as she could, Miya scanned the trail. Gray slabs of granite covered the path. Piles of rock backed up the hillside. They buried the trail and poured over its edge like giant hands had scooped up boulders and left them strewn across the trail.

Rocks rumbled above them. Dream shifted nervously. "It's fine, girl." Miya lowered the binoculars and patted the mare's neck. "The slide you're hearing is miles away. The ground is unstable in this rain."

What if the Forest Service couldn't blast them out because of the shifting ground? She had no idea how long a team with shovels would take to dig through the slide. Miya's hands shook so badly that she rested the binoculars on her thigh.

After a few moments, Miya forced herself to raise the binoculars again. Uprooted trees scattered like Lincoln Logs. Boulders had created deep furrows, which ran parallel down the mountainside and disappeared over the edge.

Miya tied Dream to a dead tree. The mare arched her neck and nickered, pulling at the lead rope. Miya touched Dream's shoulder. "I know you don't feel safe here, but I need to take a better look."

Balancing on the rocks, Miya took a few steps. The sharp edges of the granite gnawed at the soles of her boots. Miya slipped and skidded over the round rocks. She picked her way over the jagged ones. If she fell, she could break an ankle or, worse, get her foot stuck between the unforgiving boulders. The smart thing would be to turn back now, but Miya needed to see how far the rockslide extended.

Edging a few more feet forward, Miya teetered on a round rock. She gazed through the binoculars straining to see if Jake was right. To her disappointment, an ocean of gray rocks unfurled before her with no end in sight. Miya lowered the binoculars. *What will we do if Tanner gets worse or if someone gets hurt?*

A rock chuck stuck its head out from between two stones and scolded her in a loud voice. Barking with enthusiasm, Zoey leaped toward the rodent, brushing past Miya. Miya's arms windmilled as she tried to regain her balance, but it was too late.

Smack! Miya fell hard onto the rocks. Her head snapped backward, and she bit her tongue. The coppery taste of blood flooded her mouth. Grunting, Miya struggled to regain her breath.

Rock chuck forgotten, Zoey smothered Miya's face with kisses. "Stop! Stop! I'll be fine." But she wasn't. Tears of pain, frustration, and anger streamed down her cheeks.

After she had cried herself out, Miya gingerly moved her arms and legs. Her ribs hurt, but it was a dull ache, not a sharp one, so Miya rolled to her knees. She groaned as she stood. Jake had been right—there was no way around the slide.

It was time to get back. Eyes downcast, leading Dream, Miya limped into camp.

Chapter Sixteen

The first stars peeked out of an inky sky. The fire cracked and popped as a piece of wood disintegrated into a shower of sparks. Miya moved her stick so the marshmallow wouldn't burn. Marshmallows tasted best when toasted to a golden brown on all sides. She didn't like it when they were charred and crunchy.

Tanner sat beside Miya, s'more in hand. He wore Miya's jacket, zipped up to his chin. He'd also draped the fleece lining from her sleeping bag across his lap. Miya frowned as she listened to him breathe. Each breath ended with a wheeze.

Tanner nibbled at his graham cracker. After a few seconds, he held the s'more out to Miya. "I'm not hungry. Can I give this to Zoey?"

Miya laid her marshmallow on top of a Hershey bar. "No, chocolate's not good for dogs. Maybe your dad wants it."

Mr. Parker stopped pacing. "I do not. I hate to interrupt your dessert, but how do you plan to get us out of here? I have an important meeting on Thursday." He stood on a stump and waved his phone around in the air. "Still no service."

Jake reached out to Tanner. "I'll eat it." He took a bite and turned to Mr. Parker. "You may as well put your phone away. We're all ears if you have any helpful ideas."

"I'm not the guide," Mr. Parker snapped. He watched Jake take another bite of s'more. "Do we even have enough food?"

Tanner gripped the arms of his chair. "Do we, Miya?"

"We always pack extra, just in case." Miya concentrated on keeping her voice low and calm. "It's freeze-dried, so it's kind of yucky, but Zoey likes the beef stroganoff. Don't you, Zoes?" The collie whined and crowded closer to Miya.

"I'm glad there's enough." Tanner closed his eyes and leaned back in his chair.

Mentally, Miya counted the packages of freeze-dried food she'd packed. After they'd eaten all their planned meals, they had enough food to last a few days if they were careful. Then, they'd be eating a lot of fish.

"We'll be fine." Listening to Tanner struggling to breathe, she hoped she was telling the truth.

As she watched Mr. Parker staring morosely at his phone, she struggled to tamp down her anger. Didn't he realize how sick his kid was? Raising her voice slightly, Miya asked, "Is your asthma bothering you, Tanner?"

Tanner lifted one shoulder in a slight shrug. "It's fine."

Miya cleared her throat. "Mr. Parker, how do you think Tanner sounds?"

Mr. Parker pocketed his phone. He felt Tanner's forehead before replying, "Kind of wheezy, but maybe a night's sleep will help. Come on, Tanner, let's turn in. Tomorrow, we'll go fishing."

Pulling his hands up into the sleeves of her jacket, Tanner followed his dad.

An hour later, Miya and Zoey sat by the fire. Miya had offered to take the first watch. Her job was to keep the fire built up to discourage the bear if he decided to come back. They'd be in real trouble if the grizzly found a way to break into their food.

Miya transferred her attention to the darkness outside the flames. She closed her eyes and listened for the sounds of a twig snapping or the woof of a bear. All was quiet except for the usual rustle of nighttime noises.

Miya stood up and moved a few steps closer to the horses. They dozed in the shadows, heads down, tails swishing. Zoey slept peacefully, curled up in a ball beside Miya's chair.

After tossing another log onto the fire, Miya zipped up her down vest and stomped her feet. Summer was slow in arriving to the high country. Frost still crunched underfoot in the morning, and a film of ice clung to the rocks when she watered the horses at the creek.

Scooting her chair closer to the fire, Miya opened her journal. She picked up her pencil and drew the rockslide. Miya sketched skulls and skeletons hiding in the rocks and crevices. She drew a grizzly bear rearing up on his hind legs and devouring the last of their food.

The fire burned down as Miya drew, so she got up, stretched, and tossed on another log. She poked the red-orange coals with a stick. After the flames grew, Miya turned her backside toward the fire to warm it. She felt a little better now that she'd vocalized her worries. *But why*, Miya wondered, *do I always sketch my fears? Shouldn't I draw something I'm grateful for?*

Miya settled back into her chair, opened the journal, and sketched Dream and the other horses grazing in the meadow. She added Jake, standing alongside Hawk with his arm thrown over the buckskin's neck. He was smiling, so Miya shaded the dimple on his left cheek.

Turning the page, Miya quickly drew Mom, Dad, and Janelle shoveling the rocks on the trail. Behind them were outlines of a big crew of people. Miya shifted her chair so the sketch would catch the glow of the firelight. When she finished, Miya wrote OVERCOMING in block letters at the bottom of the page.

It was a good title because it conveyed a sense of moving forward and rescue. After closing the journal, Miya filled her lungs with crisp air scented with woodsmoke. She tipped her head back to gaze at the sweep of stars above her. For this single moment in time, Miya was at peace.

After breakfast the next morning, Miya set up a youth rod and reel for Tanner. "This was Jake's first fly rod. It's the perfect size for you. Here's a fishing vest and remember to wear your ballcap so you don't hook yourself. You still need a pair of polarized sunglasses to protect your eyes and help you see the fish." She raised her eyebrows at Mr. Parker. "Sunglasses were on the list."

"Do you have an extra pair?" he asked.

"Nope. Only my own. Took me two months to save up for them, so I don't loan them out." She stared pointedly at Mr. Parker's expensive pair.

He sighed. "All right. You can wear mine, Tanner, but be very careful. Whatever you do, don't drop them in the creek."

Miya suppressed a giggle and the urge to say, "Hmm, what else fell into the creek?"

Mr. Parker handed over the sunglasses, wincing as Tanner grabbed them by the lens, smearing them with fingerprints.

Clearing his throat, Mr. Parker said, "If you point us toward the pool, Miya, we can take it from there."

"I'll show you the way and if you don't need me, I'll leave." Based on her experience with taking her cousins fishing, Miya doubted Mr. Parker had the patience to untangle knots, free snags, and tie-on flies, all while avoiding the sharp barb of a novice's hook.

When they arrived at the creek bank, Mr. Parker propped his own rod against a tree and demonstrated casting to Tanner. He broke down each part of the skill and allowed Tanner to practice before moving on. After demonstrating a roll cast, Mr. Parker decided they were almost ready to start fishing for real.

"Thanks, Miya. I know you have more important things to do back at camp. I want to spend some time with Tanner, so you go ahead. We'll be back shortly."

Miya glanced around uneasily. Although Mr. Parker had informed Tanner he was knowledgeable about the outdoors, Miya hadn't seen any evidence of it. She'd promised Dad to keep both clients safe. Instead of agreeing, she asked, "Do you have your bear spray?"

"Yes." Mr. Parker nodded toward his backpack. "Over there."

"Do you mind?" Miya unzipped the front of Mr. Parker's pack and carried the canister to him. "It won't do you any good unless you can reach it quickly." She chewed her bottom lip. "Guess I'll leave now. You guys have fun."

Miya climbed the hill and chose a spot behind a tree to settle in. From her vantage point, she could see the intersection of two trails and the creek. *I never said I'd go back to camp, I only said I'd leave.*

Closing her eyes, Miya allowed the stillness of the morning to soothe the knot of tension between her shoulders. Insects hummed, and the sun shone warmly on the top of her head.

Tanner's voice carried clearly in the mountain air. "I'm in an afterschool chess club. I won a trophy."

"You have?" There was surprise in Mr. Parker's voice.

"Yep. I like chess because you don't have to talk to anybody or try to make others like you. The game is a puzzle your opponent makes up. By watching the other person's moves, you solve the puzzle and win."

"Huh," said Mr. Parker. "That's something. How did you learn to play?"

"A cool teenager who works at the afterschool club taught me to play backward. He started with checkmate cuz it's always exciting to win, and later he showed me a bunch of strategies to find my way back to the beginning."

"Impressive," Mr. Parker said as the pair moved downstream.

A delicate doe paused at the intersection of the trails. Her coat was smooth, eyes large and dark. After staring intently at Mr. Parker and Tanner, she flicked her black-tipped tail and bounded into the forest.

Chapter Seventeen

The next morning, Miya straightened and braced her hand against the small of her back. She'd only cut six logs for the fire and already had a blister on her thumb. Miya frowned at the rusty saw. She'd remind Jake to sharpen it once they got home. Miya picked up the wood and stacked it by the fire pit.

"Hey, you! Do you want me to catch Dollar so we can ride a little before lunch?"

Tanner rubbed his chest and shook his head. "No thanks, Miya."

"How about going for a walk to the creek? We can fish or wade in the water and look for neat rocks."

At the word "walk," Zoey jumped to her feet and shook. Dust, dandruff, and dog hair swirled in a small tornado around her.

Tanner peered at the creek. "No. Too far. Besides…" Tanner squinted. "It's too bright over there."

He had almost finished speaking when an ugly cough took hold. Miya tensed as Tanner struggled to breathe between coughing fits. In a few seconds, he was gasping. Tanner drew his shoulders toward his ears, trying to pull air into his lungs. Each breath ended in a high-pitched whistling sound.

Miya found herself taking deep breaths as she tried to breathe for Tanner. She ran over to the water bag hanging in the tree. Her hand shook so hard she could barely press the button for filtered water. Miya rushed back to Tanner's chair, most of the water slosh-ing over the side of the cup.

"Here's some water. Drink." Miya thrust the cup in his direction.

Tanner shook his head and pushed it away. His nostrils flared as he tried to suck in some air. Eyes, wide and panicked, Tanner slumped in his chair, his breathing quick and shallow.

Miya dropped to her knees in front of him. "Sit up straight, Tanner. You're doing fine. Stay calm."

Tanner's eyes flicked toward her, then away.

"Can you take deep breaths?" Miya gripped Tanner's hand. "When my friend Lily has an attack, she tries to breathe in through her nose, out through her mouth. Miya demonstrated. "In." She took a deep breath through her nose. "Out." She blew air from her mouth.

Pulling his hand away, Tanner shook his head. He was gasping now. His breaths came even more quickly.

Miya jumped up. "Slower, Tanner. You've got to calm down and breathe slower!"

Tanner's lips were tinged with blue. He pushed against the arms of the chair, trying to stand, but instead, he stumbled forward and fell at her feet.

Miya froze. She stared at the crumpled heap of a boy in the too-big jacket and too-short jeans. Zoey looked up to her, whined, and licked Tanner's outstretched hand.

Shaking, Miya knelt beside Tanner. She turned him over care-fully. He was breathing through his mouth, almost at a normal rate.

"Thank God, Zoey. I thought for a minute…" She closed her eyes and pinched the bridge of her nose. "I thought he was going to die."

Miya watched Tanner's skinny chest rise and fall. She touched his clammy forehead before reaching over and gently removing his glasses. After setting them on the table, Miya moistened a paper towel with cool water and dabbed at his face.

"Tanner! Hey, Tanner! Wake up! You're scaring me." She continued wiping his forehead with the paper towel. "Tanner, can you hear me?"

Tanner's eyes fluttered open. He squinted at Miya in confusion.

"It's me, Miya. You passed out."

"Oh." Tanner lay still and gazed around the camp.

After a few minutes, Miya asked, "Want to get up?"

Tanner nodded. After he sat up, he tried to shrug off Miya's coat.

"Let me help." Miya eased her coat off Tanner's thin shoulders.

"I coughed all last night." Tanner's voice was hoarse. "That's why I'm so tired today."

Miya could almost see Tanner's heart beating under his shirt. He was so pale his freckles stood out in a rust-colored spatter across his cheeks.

She waited until his breathing almost normalized before asking, "How often do you take your asthma medicine?"

"I have two inhalers." Tanner wiped beads of sweat from the side of his nose. "One is my preventer with steroids. It keeps my lungs open. I use it twice a day. I have a rescue inhaler for emergencies."

"I didn't realize how bad your asthma was." Miya sat down on the grass and pulled her knees to her chin.

Tanner glanced at Zoey. "I'm usually okay if I have my inhalers. I thought I could do this trip because Dad wanted to go fishing with me." Tanner shifted his gaze to her. "But I'm scared, Miya. I can't breathe up here."

Miya stood up and reached for Tanner's glasses. She polished them on her shirttail. "I'm scared, too."

Tanner held out his hand for the glasses. "I never passed out before. It felt like I was holding my breath underwater, and when I tried to come up for air, someone pushed me back under."

Although it was a cool morning, Miya's face grew hot. "You're doing better now. Do you want to sit over there in the sunshine?"

Pushing the glasses up on the bridge of his nose, Tanner sighed. "I have a headache. I want to go to bed." Tanner closed his eyes and wheezed. "Can you help me with my sleeping bag?"

"Of course, I can." Miya reached down to help Tanner out of his chair. "Zoey, you and your hairy body stay here."

Ignoring the collie's reproachful gaze, Miya helped Tanner to his tent. She straightened out his sleeping bag and fluffed his pillow. Tanner said it was easier for him to breathe if his head was higher, so she rolled up all the clothes she could find. She tied them with baling twine and put the bundle under Tanner's pillow.

Tanner crawled into the bag and pulled the top over him. "Thanks, Miya."

Miya knelt beside him. "I'll stay close to your tent. Call me if you need me."

Closing his eyes, Tanner nodded. Miya stared down at him. His skin was as pale as the snow that would drift across this campsite soon.

Miya backed out of the tent and dropped into a camp chair. What if Tanner had…Miya tried to push the thought out of her brain. But it persisted, returning each time fully formed. What if he had died?

Miya gagged. The sausage and pancakes she'd eaten for breakfast gurgled in her stomach. She pulled at the collar of her T-shirt. She needed air. Miya forced herself to take deep breaths. In, hold, out. In, hold, out…

After several minutes, Miya got to her feet and paced back and forth from her tent to Tanner's. What if Tanner had another asthma attack before his dad returned? What if it was worse this time?

A faint voice called from inside the tent. "Miya."

Miya threw open the flap. "What's wrong?" She didn't like the note of panic that crept into her voice, but it was getting harder and harder to pretend everything was okay.

"Nothing." Tanner looked at her with surprise. "Except I'm bored."

Sighing with relief, Miya sank, cross-legged, onto Mr. Parker's sleeping bag. She sniffed. "It stinks like dirty socks in here." One corner of Tanner's mouth turned up for an instant. "How would you like to be the one sleeping on them?"

Miya giggled. "No thanks."

She pulled off her boots and laid down on top of the sleeping bag. Miya crossed her arms behind her head and stared at the tent's ceiling. "Feeling okay?"

"For now."

The muscles in Miya's neck and shoulders relaxed. "That's good."

Miya's mind wandered. She thought about school. It started in a couple of months. "You're going into fifth grade, right? How do you like school?"

"I hate it."

The flatness in Tanner's tone took Miya by surprise. "Why?"

"Lots of reasons. My stupid asthma, for one. Mom told the principal she'd sue if he didn't make the proper accommodations for my illness." Tanner's voice was sarcastic as he repeated "accommodations for my illness" and kicked the top cover off his sleeping bag.

"Ouch! What does 'proper accommodations' mean?"

"It means that when the other kids are having fun in PE, I have to be the scorekeeper and pick up the equipment when they're done."

Miya was quiet for a minute. "That stinks. What about recess?"

"They all play football or soccer or whatever. I don't even know the rules."

Glancing out the door, Miya saw Zoey sitting a few feet away, head cocked to one side, peering inside the tent. Miya sat up. "You're smart. Things must be okay in the classroom."

"The teachers are mostly nice. The kids, not so much. Last year, we played board games every Friday. Not chess. Dumb ones like Sorry. Anyway, no one ever chose me. So, it was the same thing each week—I'd put my head down on my desk and wait until the teacher assigned me to a group. I tried to act like everybody else... you know, joke around and stuff." Tanner let out a long sigh. "But all the time, I knew the others thought I was the weird kid and wished they weren't stuck with me."

Miya swallowed and waited. She needed to make sure her voice was steady when she answered. Tanner might feel worse if he thought she felt sorry for him.

"Newsflash, Tanner. I used to get bullied, too. The kids called me Mega Miya cuz I was so heavy."

Tanner sat up in surprise. "But Miya, you're not fat."

Miya glanced down at her stomach. She'd tightened her belt another notch this morning. "I'm not *as* fat, but you know how some kids will say anything to make your life miserable."

"Yeah," agreed Tanner. "You got that right."

Miya tossed her braid over her shoulder. "You want me to tell you a secret about how to get through it? The bullying, I mean?"

"Yeah, of course I do."

"Okay. Here it comes." Miya lowered her voice. "Set up a cache."

Tanner sat forward on his sleeping bag. "A cache? What's that?"

"A few years ago, I climbed into a cave and found a mountain lion cache. There was a baby bighorn sheep skull, a cub's paw, the black tip of a mule deer's tail, and some other stuff."

Miya stared at the side of the tent, remembering that day. She recalled the sound of rain dripping from the ceiling of the cave, the gritty sandstone, and the strong smell of cat pee.

"I thought maybe the stuff in the cave was important to the mountain lion. So, I decided to set up my own cache with things that were important to me. In my desk drawer, I have my first barrel racing check, my first sculpture, a few other things, and lately…" Her cheeks reddened. "My journal."

Tanner frowned. "How does that help with bullying?"

Miya looked out the door of the tent, where Zoey stood guard. "When I have a bad day, I call my dog, and we go up to my cache. I pick up my barrel racing check and think that no matter what the other kids say, my horse and I are a winning team." Miya smiled to herself. "Or I hold up my sculpture and realize I created something with my own two hands." She shrugged. "After a while, I start to feel better."

"I like it." Tanner stood up. "Let's start now. I need something to help me remember the day I rode Dollar forever and ever and ever." Tanner flopped back down on the sleeping bag, pretending to be exhausted.

Miya reached for her boots. "You made it over a 10,000-foot pass and survived a grizzly bear coming into camp. How many other kids can say that happened to them this summer?"

A few minutes later, Miya watched Tanner wander around the camp, pick up several small rocks, study them, and drop them back into the dirt. Finally, he sat down in a chair, breathing in short wheezes.

"Rocks won't work," he said. "Not for the first thing in my cache."

"Why?" Miya picked up a small, layered stone. "We might be able to find some petrified wood."

"No. The very first thing for my cache needs to show bravery." Tanner struck a pose, arms bent at ninety degrees, showing Miya his muscles.

Miya tried not to giggle at the sight of his small biceps. With a grin, she switched her attention to the horses. "I could pull a few strands of Dollar's tail. You were brave when you rode him over the pass."

"That could be the second thing."

Zoey ambled over to her bowl and crunched a mouthful of dry dog food. "I could take a picture of you and Zoey and send it to you when we get service. She's done lots of brave stuff."

Tanner shook his head. "Maybe for the third thing."

Miya sat down next to Tanner. She watched his shoulders rise and fall as he struggled to breathe the thin mountain air. "You should take a nap. We can work on this later after you feel better."

Tanner crossed his arms over his chest. His eyebrows drew together in a stubborn V. "Not until I find my first thing."

Miya circled the camp. "How about this?" She pointed to a small tuft of brown fur. "It's grizzly hair from when he rubbed against this tree, trying to reach the panniers up there. Grizzles are strong and super brave." Miya worked the hair free from the bark. It was coarser than she expected.

Tanner reached out and took the fur. He rubbed it between his fingers, nodded, picked up a sandwich bag, and sealed the hair inside.

"This will work." He grinned at her. "You don't need a cache because you're brave, Miya, like a grizzly bear."

Miya shook her head. She didn't have the heart to tell Tanner she wasn't a bit brave. She was only pretending to be.

"C'mon. Let's get you back in bed."

After leaving Tanner's tent, Miya split wood instead of trying to cut the smaller logs with the rusty saw. She set a log on its end, planted both feet, and whap! Miya brought the ax down as hard as she could. The shock of metal on wood vibrated up to her shoulders. She needed to calm down and drop the ax instead of swinging it so hard, but the gnawing worry inside her made Miya want to pound on something.

After she had split three logs into eight smaller pieces, Miya listened at the door of Tanner's tent. Hearing only silence, she bent down and peered inside. Tanner's back was turned toward her. He seemed to be sleeping, so Miya tiptoed away.

Restlessly, Miya glanced around camp, undecided about which job to tackle first. A half-empty water bag hung near the kitchen panniers. She needed to take the bag down to the creek and refill it. That way, there would be plenty of time for the water to run through the filter before lunch. As Miya stretched up to untie the bag, she noticed the peanut butter jar from the sandwiches Jake had made that morning.

Maybe Tanner would be hungry enough to eat a couple of no-bake cookies. She could use the peanut butter to make a batch. Miya rummaged around and found oatmeal, canned milk, and cocoa.

Before getting involved with the cookies, she checked on Tanner again. Miya crept into his tent. She froze as the plastic floor crackled underfoot. Miya stared at the small form huddled in the sleeping bag. Was Tanner still breathing? Heart pounding, Miya tiptoed closer. Seconds ticked by as she remained motionless, willing Tanner's chest to move up and down. Finally, he drew a shallow breath. Relieved, Miya turned, wishing that Jake and Mr. Parker would hurry back.

"Miya?" Tanner's leg jerked as he woke. "Why are you back again?"

"Sorry. I wanted to make sure you were okay."

"I'm fine. I just need sleep."

"Right." Miya nodded. "I won't bother you anymore if you promise to call me if you start to feel bad."

Tanner punched the bundle of clothes under his pillow. "I promise."

Chapter Eighteen

Miya left the tent. Grabbing the ax, she ticked off the chores in her head. First, split three more logs. Second, refill the water bag. Third, brush the horses. Miya checked the meadow to reassure herself that all the horses were grazing peacefully. Her eyes traveled to the mountain behind them. She blew out a long, jagged breath. There was…no, there *might* be one other trail out of here. Miya froze, staring at the sheer rock wall dotted with stunted trees. At the very top was a snow-covered peak called Smith's Summit.

Last summer, wolves or bears pushed a few of their cows up toward the Summit. Miya and her dad had found the cattle before they strayed too far. Although they'd only ridden a few miles, things quickly turned treacherous. Floods had devoured large sections of the trail, forcing them to ride along the steep side of the mountain.

Miya remembered seeing twisted junipers with branches gnarled like witches' fingers. The other trees were mostly fire-blackened. They creaked a warning as she rode by.

Her dad had ridden up to the pass once as a teenager. He pointed out a few of the lower landmarks to Miya. A dull gray rock they called the Flatiron. A u-shaped bowl where the mountain had sloughed off hundreds of years ago. An archway of red rock with a heart-shaped hole in the middle.

No way was she going back there. Ever. And besides, although the old timers told stories of some brave crazy people making it over the pass, no one ever attempted it now. Not even the Forest Service guys. Too rough. Too steep. Too dangerous. With a sigh, Miya abandoned the idea of anyone riding out over Smith's Summit. They'd have to be patient and wait for help.

At dusk, Jake and Mr. Parker rode into camp. An icy wind blew in on their heels, rattling the sides of the canvas cook tent. Miya turned the heat up under the pot of water. At this altitude, it took forever to boil. Miya broke the spaghetti noodles in half and dropped them in when the water bubbled.

Miya dumped a bag of salad mix in a bowl. Usually, she picked out the big chunks of lettuce core before serving it, but tonight, Miya tossed in the whole thing and poured all the dressing on top of it. She forced herself to smile as Mr. Parker slid stiffly off his horse.

Miya planned to wait until after supper to tell him about Tanner's asthma attack. She hated it when people sprang bad news on her when she was hungry and cold. But, as she looked at Tanner slumped in his chair, Miya wondered if she should wait any longer.

Jake stood in the shadows, holding the horses. Though she wanted to hug him, she petted Hawk instead and whispered, "Worried about your mom?"

There was no hint of the usual easy-going laughter in his eyes. "Yeah. Logically, I know there's a ninety-eight percent chance she's fine. It's the other two percent I can't stop thinking about."

"I know. Me, too."

Miya squeezed his hand before he clucked to the horses and led them away.

Head down, Miya dragged herself back to the Coleman stove and resumed her post. "How was fishing?"

"Great!" Mr. Parker scrolled through his phone and showed her several pictures. "Trout were biting like crazy. It was almost a waste of time to tie on a fly." He laughed and looked at Tanner. "I want you to go with us tomorrow. Do you think you'll feel up to it?"

Tanner shrugged. "Maybe."

"Supper's in twenty minutes if you want to put your stuff away." Miya turned toward Tanner, raising her eyebrows. He nodded back.

Miya could feel Mr. Parker's gaze as he looked between her and Tanner. Tanner stared into the fire while Miya concentrated on stirring the spaghetti.

"All right." Mr. Parker pushed back his ball cap and turned toward the tent.

An hour later, Miya twirled the spaghetti around on her fork, let it drop back into the pile, and twisted the noodles again. Mr. Parker droned on about fishing the creeks and pools under the falls. Jake had eaten quickly and now sat, almost motionless, holding his empty plate and staring into the darkness.

Tanner huddled next to the fire. Like hers, his plate was mostly untouched. He'd managed a few bites of French bread but hadn't eaten any of his spaghetti.

Tanner held the plate up. "Can I put this in Zoey's bowl?"

Miya opened her mouth to respond, but instead of answering Tanner's question, she blurted out, "I thought Tanner was going to die today!" Whoa! That wasn't what she'd meant to say at all.

"Miya!" Tanner glared at her.

"Sorry." She looked down at the lump of congealed sauce and noodles in front of her. "I know you're trying to act all tough for your dad, but I'm scared. He needs to understand how sick you are."

Mr. Parker's face froze. He turned to Tanner. "Did you have an asthma attack or something? You said you could get by without your inhalers for a few days."

"He can't." Miya stood up and slid her uneaten spaghetti into a sandwich bag. She stomped back and grabbed Tanner's plate. Lettuce scattered as she slammed it down on the table. "He passed out today. I've seen people faint before, but this was a hundred times scarier because he couldn't breathe."

Mr. Parker's jaw dropped. He stared at Tanner in disbelief. "You passed out?"

"Yes!" Miya was nearly shouting now, but she couldn't stop herself. "Passed out, fainted, keeled over! When will you understand that this trip isn't about you and fishing? It's about Tanner, and he needs your help!"

Tomato sauce, oregano, green pepper. The smell of spaghetti was overpowering. Miya gagged and turned away. Suddenly, Jake was beside her, pulling her into his arms. Miya melted into him, burying her face in the soft denim of his shirt and inhaling the smell of horses and woodsmoke.

"Shh, shh," Jake rubbed her back and made the same soothing sounds he used with a skittish colt.

After a minute, Miya lifted her head and whispered, "Tanner could have died! I was alone! All I could do was watch."

Jake spoke softly. "You both made it, and you're not alone now. Why don't you tell us what happened, step by step."

Haltingly, Miya and Tanner recounted the story. When they finished, Mr. Parker rubbed his face with both hands. He grasped the arms of his camp chair and pulled it closer to Tanner's.

"I'm sorry I wasn't here for you guys. How does your mom handle an asthma attack?"

"I don't usually have an attack if I have my inhalers." He bit his lip. "It started last night, and I couldn't breathe very well today."

They all stared at him.

"I still can't."

Tanner's wheezing was louder. It echoed and bounced around in Miya's brain. She hoped she hadn't stressed him out with her yelling.

At the edge of the meadow, the peak of Smith's Summit loomed. Illuminated by the rising moon, its ghostly face mocked her. Miya gazed at it, wishing she could be a hero and ride out over it for help. But she couldn't. Not even for Tanner.

Mr. Parker snapped his fingers. "Maybe breathing steam will help. Tanner, we need to reduce the inflammation in your lungs and clear up the congestion. We used a vaporizer when you were a baby and had a cold. Why don't we make one now?"

Mr. Parker pointed at Jake. "Jake, fill a pot of water. The one you use for washing dishes. Miya, find a towel. One that's big enough to cover Tanner's head and shoulders.

As Miya hurried toward her tent to find a towel, she glanced back toward the pair. Mr. Parker stood with his arm around Tanner's shoulders, talking quietly.

Fifteen minutes later, Tanner looked like a navy-blue ghost. He had a towel draped over his head as he hunched above the steaming water. Mr. Parker tapped him on the shoulder. "Do you think it's helping?"

"Don't know." Tanner's reply was muffled.

Miya chewed her thumbnail. The makeshift vaporizer had to help. Mr. Parker said Tanner's breathing should improve after ten or fifteen minutes. All they needed to do was make it through a few more days, and surely, someone would rescue them.

"Can I be done? My eyelashes are dripping."

As though performing a magic trick, Mr. Parker pulled the towel off Tanner's head. "How do you feel?"

Tanner shrugged and slipped on his glasses. "Maybe a little better?"

"I'll get some more water." Jake picked up another pot. "We might need to do this again later."

"Good idea," Mr. Parker said. He sat down in a camp chair and rubbed his forehead.

As the wind stirred the trees, dark shadows skirted across the sky. Miya shivered and pulled up her hood. The temperature had fallen at least ten degrees since sunset. She started gathering the dishes.

Behind her, Tanner coughed—a dry cough that ended with a wheezing sound. Miya swung around. "Tanner?"

He shook his head and coughed harder.

"This is exactly how you sounded before your attack this morning!" Miya threw the silverware on the table. A noodle was stuck between the tines of a fork. Jake dropped the pot and ran to Tanner's side.

Mr. Parker knelt in front of him. "Sit up straight, buddy." He pushed gently on Tanner's shoulder. "You need to get air in those lungs."

Tanner leaned back against his chair. His eyes were wide, his breaths short and shallow.

Miya knelt beside Mr. Parker. She rubbed Tanner's arm. "Be calm. Think about your cache."

Tanner's eyes moved to Miya's face. He nodded. His breathing slowed.

Miya climbed unsteadily to her feet. "Now that you're feeling a little better, I'll head to the creek and get water for coffee. Maybe Jake will whip up one of his special cowboy coffees. Lily told me that caffeine helps her asthma sometimes."

Without waiting for an answer, Miya grabbed the coffee pot and hurried down the path. She scuffed through the pine needles, thinking about Tanner, wishing she weren't terrified of the mountain. On the way back, the water sloshed onto her boots. Each time the water splashed, it murmured, "Coward, coward."

"Maybe Jake could ride out," Miya whispered the words. She shook her head. That wouldn't work. Jake had no idea what to look for on Smith's Summit. After riding with her dad, Miya would recognize landmarks on the first part of the trail.

In her mind, Miya replayed the scene. She saw the desperate panic in Tanner's eyes. She heard his harsh gasps for breath. She felt the clamminess of his skin. *I need to help Tanner, but do I have what it takes to make this ride?*

Miya sat on a rock and searched the night sky. Leaning against a tree, she remembered her family's camping trip when she was little. Long after her usual bedtime, she, Mom, and Dad snuggled into sleeping bags, and they all looked for the constellations. Miya's favorite had been Ursa Minor, Little Bear, because it held the North Star. The star that guided travelers home.

Now, after locating the North Star, Miya swore she'd never allow Tanner to die because of her fears. Tomorrow, she'd find a way home. She had no choice; Tanner was running out of time.

Chapter Nineteen

An hour later, with Tanner tucked into his tent, Miya finally returned to the dishes. Mr. Parker approached, picked up a dish towel, and dried a plate. He placed the plate in the kitchen pannier and reached for another. After wiping circles around the rim for several seconds, he cleared his throat. "I've been talking to Jake."

Keeping her voice neutral, Miya said, "Have you?"

"He told me how dangerous the ride over Smith Summit will be. I know it's going to be especially hard for you."

Squeezing the dishrag into a small ball beneath the soapy water, Miya asked, "What do you mean by 'especially hard for me'?"

"Jake said the trail is treacherous. I've watched you these past couple of days. It's easy to see how terrified of heights you are. It's called acrophobia."

Rinsing a bowl, Miya shrugged. "I might have acro... whatever. Yes, I'm scared of heights, but that doesn't matter. All that matters is getting help for Tanner."

"Thank you for that." Mr. Parker sighed and handed a pan to Miya. "I know you think I'm a terrible father, and maybe I am. After the divorce, Tanner's mother made it so hard for me to see him that I basically gave up. It was easier than dealing with all the arguments and manipulations.

Miya could understand that. Most of her friends came from blended families. They told never-ending stories about parents and stepparents fighting constantly.

Mr. Parker continued. "When I do get Tanner for a visit, it feels awkward. I don't know how to act around kids. I'm an only child, so I don't even have nieces or nephews to practice on."

Losing patience with his excuses, Miya blew the bangs off her forehead and faced Mr. Parker. "You were a kid once, weren't you? It's not rocket science. Play basketball or video games. Go out for ice cream. Make up knock-knock jokes."

Nodding, Mr. Parker said, "I'm starting to get it. Since Tanner is so sick, I realize how much time I've wasted." He cleared his throat and patted her clumsily on the shoulder. "So, thanks, Miya, for attempting this trip."

He folded the dish towel into fourths. "I better check on him. See you tomorrow."

Tiny splinters of sleet fell from the sky, tapping Miya's hat. Miya and Jake huddled under a blanket, staring into the fire. Miya rocked back and forth. She clutched her journal to her chest.

Jake reached over and gently pried her fingers off the book. He set it down on the seat of a camp chair and held Miya's hand.

"I'm afraid for you to go."

"I'm scared, too."

"So don't do it. A few days ago, your anxiety wouldn't let you lead the trip over Wildcat Pass. How are you going to make it over the Summit? Think about it. The Summit is much higher. The trail is either gone or blocked by downfalls and slides."

Jake squeezed her hand. "What sense does it make to risk your life? You'll have to turn around anyway when you can't get through. You should wait for the Forrest Service to get here."

Miya flinched. Jake might be right, but his words still stung. He'd always encouraged her, yet now he pointed out obstacles and acted like she couldn't overcome them.

"You may be right, but I have to try."

Jake jumped to his feet. "What if you break a leg or fall off the mountain? I won't be there to help you. One mistake, Miya, one mistake, and you die."

Miya stood up slowly. "Thank you very much for the vote of confidence. I have ridden in the back county once or twice...or all my life. Maybe the odds are stacked against me, but at least Dream and Zoey believe in me."

As the silence grew between them, Miya took a breath and gazed at the night sky. The sleet pricked her skin with icy dots. The North Star was gone, hidden behind the clouds. "I won't let Tanner down. Or Dad. He trusted me to take care of the people on this trip. He's counting on me, too."

Miya picked up her journal. "My mind's made up. I'm leaving in the morning."

Although Zoey lay curled up beside her, Miya shivered in her sleeping bag. To keep her mind off the mountain, she listed the things she'd pack in her saddlebags tomorrow. Dream didn't need to carry any extra weight on the long, steep ride out.

Water bottle, granola bars, flashlight, matches, a bag of dry dog food. Her pocketknife, of course. Should she pack the first aid kit? It was light but bulky. Still debating, Miya drifted off to sleep.

Jake stuck his head in her tent at 5:00 the next morning. "Hey, I gave Tanner my coat and got yours back. You're gonna need it." He tossed the coat to her, pulled up the hood of his sweatshirt, and jammed his hands into the front pockets of his hoodie.

Miya sat up. The freezing air hit her with a smack.

"I fed Dream and started the coffee. It's going to be a long day. You need to leave by first light."

Bracing herself against the cold, Miya stood up and pulled her clothes over her long underwear. She packed her saddlebags. Miya tried to shove the first aid kit in, but it wouldn't fit unless she took out Zoey's dog food.

Miya held the bag in one hand and the first aid kit in the other. Miya would feed Zoey an extra big breakfast this morning, and her dog would be fine for the day, but what if something happened, and they had to spend the night on the mountain?

Miya knelt and hugged Zoey. Leaving the first aid kit on her sleeping bag, she shrugged into her coat and stepped outside.

During the night, the sleet had changed to snow. The snow wasn't the white, fluffy kind that decorated Christmas cards. It was fine and grainy and still falling lightly.

Miya heard Jake talk to Dream as he brushed her. Despite last night's argument, she wished he was going with her today.

After emptying a pack of instant oatmeal into a bowl, Miya poured boiling water over it. By the dim light of the lantern, she watched the orange dots darken and float in the cereal. They were supposed to be peaches, but the flecks were nothing but tasteless confetti.

Miya forced herself to take a bite. The oatmeal was already getting cold. She dumped it in the fire. Miya picked up her saddlebags and headed to where Jake was saddling Dream.

Avoiding her eyes, Jake finished buckling the breast collar before he spoke. "I wish I could go for you."

Miya flexed her reddened fingers and wiggled her toes in her wet boots. She'd give anything to climb back into her sleeping bag, doze off, and let Jake handle the whole thing.

They both knew she wouldn't do that. Miya threw her arms around Jake and hugged him tightly, resting her head against his chest and closing her eyes. For a minute, the two stood motionless as the snow fell heavily in the pines around them.

Jake touched her cheek. "Sorry I came on so strong last night, but I'm scared for you."

Miya stiffened. She didn't want Jake to start verbalizing her worries. "We've already talked about—"

"Let me finish. Even though I'm worried, if anyone can find a way over the pass, it'll be you. You got this, Miya. I believe in you."

"Even with all this stupid anxiety stuff?" Miya hated that her voice wavered.

"Especially with all this anxiety stuff."

Jake set her away and smiled. "When you see her, tell Mom we're on to her. Some people will do anything to get out of work."

Miya laughed as she hugged Jake one more time. She called for Zoey and stepped up on Dream.

"Wait! Miya! Wait!" Miya turned to see Tanner running toward her. Jake's jacket reached to his knees, and the arms flapped like the wings of a baby bird.

"Whoa, Tanner. Stop. You don't need to be running, and you don't need to be out in this cold. You'll have another attack."

Miya slid off Dream and put an arm around his shoulders. Tanner's words came out in a rush. "I didn't want to miss you. I heard you and Jake talking last night."

Miya zipped his jacket higher. "Slow down. Why didn't you want to miss me?"

Tanner wiggled his hand out of the cuff of Jake's jacket and held out the bag of grizzly fur. "I wanted to give you this."

Puzzled, Miya asked, "Don't you need it for your cache?"

"Of course, I do." Tanner waved the bag at her. "But after you take it over the mountain, when I need to be brave, I'll remember how you did something to help instead of standing around scared."

Mr. Parker held his hand out to Miya. "Thanks again, Miya." He unzipped Jake's jacket and motioned for Tanner to take it off. "Jake needs his coat. You can wear mine."

Mya tucked the bag into her vest pocket and stepped back on Dream. "Wish me luck." She waved and headed toward the trail.

Chapter Twenty

The snow squeaked under Dream's hooves as Miya rode east toward the mountain. Miya watched the first light appear above the treetops. The sunrise painted a pale watercolor of yellow and orange streaks across the sky.

Dream reached the stream halfway across the meadow. She put her head down and snuffled at the snow-covered ice.

"Thirsty, girl?"

Miya got off, found a heavy rock, and flung it down. The thin glaze of ice splintered. Miya kicked a few glass-like pieces aside. She threw another rock, making a bigger hole in the ice. Dream drank deeply, occasionally lifting her head to gaze into the woods.

Zoey jumped into the creek beside Dream, splashing and barking. The collie lapped her fill of water and bounded up on the other bank, tail waving, inviting Miya to play. Miya laughed and shook her head at Zoey. "Sorry, girl, I don't have time to throw snowballs for you today."

The wind stung Miya's eyes, and tears formed at their corners. She wiped them away with the back of her glove. "I hope those clouds lift before we get to the top. Finding our way through this fog will be hard." Miya's mind conjured an image of an icy gray curtain obscuring the edge of a cliff as Dream plunged over it, screaming with terror.

"Stop it!" Miya said the words out loud, although she could barely hear them over the thundering of her heart. "Stop it, Miya. Get a grip. For Tanner."

Miya mounted Dream and resumed her journey. Dream tried to drift toward camp, but Miya shifted her weight and directed the paint to the game trail at the edge of the meadow. "I know you'd rather be with your friends, but today, I need you to help me find my way."

A half mile later, Miya entered the forest. Trees shrouded in snow blocked the weak light. From deep in the woods, Miya heard a sharp crack as a branch gave way under the weight of the snow. Miya and Dream both jumped.

As they headed deeper into the timber, Miya fought the dread that slithered down her throat and coiled in the pit of her stomach. She looked down at her saddle horn, concentrating on the tiny stitches encircling it.

Suddenly, Dream stopped. Miya looked ahead—a fallen pine tree blocked the trail. Its branches were broken. Its roots twisted like the fingers of an arthritic old woman.

Miya studied the path beyond the pine, just out of reach. She backed Dream up three steps, turned her off the trail, and worked her way around the downed timber. The blackened trunks of the trees crisscrossed each other, creating a maze of nearly impassable tangles.

Dream stepped across a small tree. She hesitated at the next one. Knife-like pieces of broken branches stuck out along the entire side of the trunk. Miya worried Dream would get cut if she tried to cross it, so she backed up and searched for another route.

A path ahead looked promising until Miya figured out yet another tree had it blocked. The barrier was at least three feet high and two feet wide. A few splintered branches stuck out from the trunk like giant prehistoric teeth, but there was a spot between them wide enough for Dream to jump—if Miya dared.

The landing could be a problem. Miya stood in her stirrups, searching for holes, slippery rocks, or roots that would trip Dream when she touched down on the other side. It was impossible to tell from where she sat because the ground was covered with snow.

Miya slid off Dream and hoisted herself up onto the downed tree. Unable to find a good grip on the slippery trunk, she fell in a heap on the other side. Miya's knee slammed against a rock.

"Ouch!" She rubbed it. "That hurt. And I still have a bruise on my other knee from that awful barrel run the other night."

Zoey raced under the tree and ran up to Miya. She laid a paw on Miya's chest and whined.

"I'm okay, girl." Miya waited for the pain to subside. After a minute, she heaved herself to her feet. Miya kicked away the rocks and branches that littered the ground.

After glancing at Dream waiting on the other side of the tree, Miya decided not to climb over the slippery trunk again. Instead, she crouched down and crawled through the space where the roots held up the tree. When Miya got to the other side, she was covered in dirt. She spat out sand and pine needles.

As Miya brushed herself off, she explained the situation to Dream. "It's pretty clear on the other side. But since we're in timber, the ground is frozen. Watch out when you land, or you'll slip and fall." She finger-combed Dream's mane, tugging at the tangles. If the horse went down, Dream or Miya could break a leg. Jake's worst nightmares would come true. Yet what choice did she have?

Miya led Dream to a rock and climbed on top of it, still favoring her sore knee. She turned her horse toward the tree. "We've got this." Miya tried to reassure herself as well as Dream.

Dream sensed Miya's hesitation and backed away from the tree.

"Throw your heart over the fence. The rest of you will follow." The quote from a poster in her homeroom sprang into her mind. Some guy named Vincent Peale said it. Miya understood the words better now. For weeks, she'd been building a fence in her head. Her fears existed on one side, hopes and dreams on the other.

After taking a deep breath, Miya squeezed her legs. Dream loped toward the tree. As the mare got closer, her strides shortened. Miya felt Dream's uneasiness. She tapped her horse with her heels. "This fence can't stop us." Miya refused to look down at the slippery ground, the thick trunk, or the sharp branches. Instead, she concentrated on the patch of blue sky beyond. She felt Dream gather herself, push off with her powerful hindquarters, and sail over the tree.

Dream landed so hard on the other side that Miya pitched forward and the saddlehorn poked her in the stomach. She barely noticed. Miya blew out the breath she'd been holding and looked back at the tree. "We did it, Dream. We made it over our first big obstacle."

Half an hour later, Miya and Dream worked their way back up to the trail. Miya got down and checked Dream for cuts and scratches. Satisfied, she stood up and rubbed her mare's forehead. "I'm glad we left early. It took us an hour to go three feet."

Leaving the woods behind, Miya checked her watch. 8:00. Considering all the backtracking they'd done, 8:00 wasn't too bad. After about a mile of following the game trail, Dream slid down the bank and landed alongside the edge of the creek. As Dream picked her way through the rocks and driftwood, Miya relaxed in her saddle. Her neck cracked as she rolled her head from side to side.

Sunlight sparkled on the creek. The water flowed, giving no hint of the strong current underneath. Miya knew the creek would narrow and become treacherous later. She remembered riding beside it the last time, watching the water rush by and tumble over the falls.

A coyote yipped. Another answered with barking and howling. Dream's ears pricked up. Miya searched the hills for a glimpse of gray-brown color against the snow. Zoey growled deep in her throat.

"Hush, Zoey. They're just talking."

The game trail twisted around a log and disappeared into the water. The shallows of the creek brimmed with minnows. At times, Miya lost sight of the trail, but after searching, she always managed to spot the hoofprints of deer and elk.

"We've been on this part of the trail for forty-five minutes. I think we walked along the creek for nearly an hour last time." Miya nervously chewed on her saddle string. "I can't be sure. I wasn't paying enough attention." She scanned the foothills on the west side. "I need to find two red rocks that look like chimneys. That's where the trail goes over the bank."

Staring at the landscape, Miya thought, *Easy, right?* Or not. Everywhere she looked, there were chimney-shaped rocks.

A wall of willows stood across the creek. Their yellow leaves rippled in the breeze. Miya knew willows loved the swamp. She pictured them growing in the deep black bog near the opposite bank. If she picked the wrong spot to cross, the bog could suck Dream in. Miya had seen it happen to a cow once. She shuddered. Her insides were tied up in a knot of worry.

As she rode along, Miya considered each group of red rocks. To her right, she saw two chimney-shaped formations. Could those be the ones? Should she try to cross the creek here? Miya stared down the trail and saw two more red rocks standing beyond the curve.

After glancing at her watch, Miya realized she and Dream had followed this path for an hour and twenty minutes. The knot in her stomach tightened. Had she come too far? When she was watching birds and daydreaming, did she miss the spot? Should she turn around and double-check?

Forcing herself to take a deep breath, Miya tried to think. They'd passed the falls a while ago. If she backtracked and were wrong, she'd lose even more time—time Tanner didn't have. Miya imagined him back at camp, fighting for each breath and counting on her.

The saddle string tasted salty as Miya bit down hard. She wished her dad was here to make the decision. She'd love to relinquish control of this whole trip. What should she do? Go on or turn back?

Sighing, Miya checked her watch for what seemed like the thirtieth time. "We'll ride a little longer, Dream. If I don't see anything familiar in the next fifteen minutes, we'll turn around."

After setting the timer on her watch, Miya and Dream started up the trail. Her shoulders tense, Miya searched every rock and crevice. She spotted a cave high above her. *Have I seen that cave before? Maybe…but it looks just like a hundred other caves I've seen.*

Thirteen minutes passed. Fourteen. *Beep, beep.* The alarm sounded. Fifteen minutes were up.

"Time's up." As she started to turn Dream around, Zoey darted up the bank and out of sight. "Zoey, come back!" Miya yelled. "Why do dogs have to chase every shadow that moves? Zoey, you better not be chasing a bear!"

Miya expected Zoey to give up on what she was chasing and race back, but after several seconds, the collie hadn't returned.

"Come on, Dream, let's go find her." Rounding the bend, Miya saw Zoey stationed at the bottom of a tree while a squirrel scolded her from above.

"Zoey, quit messing around. We have to—"

Miya stopped talking. She nearly stopped breathing. Her eyes widened. Two chimney-shaped spires pointed heavenward on the other side of the creek.

Relief loosened the knot in her belly as Miya recognized the reddish rock formation.

"There it is, Dream! Let's cross the creek!"

As the mare navigated the slick rocks on the bottom, Miya slipped her feet out of the stirrups and held them high. Her boots had just started to dry out from the snow this morning, but her socks were still damp from where the moisture had seeped in around the duct tape.

When they reached the opposite bank, Miya slipped her feet back into the stirrups and looked at the trail. Animal tracks were pressed into the dirt. Coyote, deer, elk, and bear all had recently crossed here.

Dream's hooves squelched in the mud. The mare put her head down, touching the black goo with her nose. She snorted.

Miya tapped Dream with her heels. "C'mon Dream. It's just mud."

Dream snorted again and jumped forward. She landed on a patch of grass growing in the middle of the swamp. Miya's sore knee banged against a spindly aspen.

"Ouch! Not the knee again!" Dream flicked an ear and lurched forward. Arching her back with a giant twist, she sailed over the rest of the bog and landed hard on solid ground.

"Oof," Miya said as her rear end hit the saddle with a thump.

None of it mattered—her knee, her butt, the headache lodged at the base of her skull. She had found the chimney-shaped rocks and was about to climb the mountain beyond.

Chapter Twenty-one

Twisting in the saddle, Miya tied her jacket behind her. It was late morning. The sun beamed down, warm and golden on her shoulders. A few sprigs of Indian paintbrush clung to the hillside. Russet-colored bushes threaded through the brown grass. Below her, the willows whispered goodbye as Miya left them behind.

The mountain ahead rose nearly straight up out of the foothills. Sage green chutes led into the dark timber. At the very top, hidden by dark clouds, stood Smith's Summit.

Miya studied the gray curtain of clouds concealing the pass. She pictured blinding snow. Slippery ground. Rockslides. Timber so thick that it swallowed her up.

She touched her vest pocket—the one that held the grizzly fur. Miya thought about Tanner, about how he never complained about being cold or wet or struggling to breathe. "I'll concentrate on what I can do. Which is start up the mountain. One step at a time."

After another mile, the trail forked. Both paths headed in the same direction, so Miya chose the left fork because it seemed the more well-traveled. Her mare walked along, swinging her head in an easy rhythm that matched her gait. Miya rubbed her knee and breathed deeply, trying to relax.

Without warning, Dream snorted and stiffened. The mare held her head high and stared at the trail in front of her. Miya craned her neck, trying to see what Dream was upset about. "What is it, girl?"

Miya spotted a dog-like animal peeking around the switchback. A coyote. It was about Zoey's size and shape but much skinnier.

"It's just a coyote, Dream. You've seen a bunch of them."

Dream shifted uneasily. Her nostrils flared. Miya touched the mare with her heels. "C'mon, let's go. He'll leave."

Dream shook her head and snorted. Miya nudged the mare forward. "He won't hurt you."

The animal stood still, mouth open, ears up, staring at them as they approached. Miya watched for a flick of his tail, a shake of his head, a yawn, a growl, any usual coyote behavior, but the coyote only watched...and waited.

"You're right, Dream. That thing's acting creepy. Why doesn't he run away?"

From behind her, Zoey growled—a low, menacing sound.

Although the hairs on the back of Miya's neck stood up, a coyote couldn't stop her. She clucked to Dream and squeezed her legs. When they got a few feet closer, Miya waved her arms and yelled, "Hey, you! Go back to your den!" She clapped her hands and smacked her thigh. "Go on home now."

Zoey growled again. The coyote turned and, like a puff of gray smoke, disappeared down the trail.

"It's okay, Zoes." Miya blew out her breath and settled back in her saddle. "He's gone."

Seconds later, Dream snorted. The mare swung her head toward the woods above them. Miya watched the trees and glimpsed a flash of reddish-gray. "He's back? Seriously, what's going on with that thing?" Miya urged Dream forward. "Let's get out of here. "She wished they could gallop away and leave the coyote behind, but the trail was too steep and rocky for anything but a cautious walk.

The coyote materialized on a ridge above Dream. Zoey barked, so the coyote vanished. But in a heartbeat, he reappeared. Silent as a ghost, the coyote stalked them. He kept pace with Dream, weaving in and out of the shadows, fading into darkness, before reemerging to watch as they passed by underneath.

Miya unbuckled her saddlebag and pulled out the bear spray. She tilted her face into the wind. If the coyote attacked from the front, she'd be out of luck. She'd end up spraying herself and Dream. Miya rubbed her finger along the plastic button as she considered the other drawback of bear spray—the coyote had to be close for it to work.

"Go away!" Miya screamed at the coyote. The coyote disappeared. Miya sighed with relief.

But then, with a snarl and a flash of teeth, the coyote launched itself at Zoey. Her collie yipped in surprise and tried to twist away as the coyote bit down on the scruff of her neck. Zoey yelped and stumbled forward, slamming into Dream. Dream kicked back hard.

Miya heard a second yelp, higher pitched than Zoey's. She turned in time to see the coyote stagger backward, retreating a few steps.

Miya bailed off Dream, jumped over Zoey, and stood in front of her dog, arms extended straight out in front of her. She trembled as she clutched the can of bear spray. The coyote shook himself and advanced—head down, yellow eyes gleaming, creeping forward on silent paws.

"Wait for it," Miya cautioned herself.

The coyote was close now, so close that she could almost see spit dripping off its razor-sharp canines. As it took another step forward, Miya tightened her grip on the can and pulled back on the button of the bear spray.

A cloud of orange particles floated in the air. The mist engulfed the coyote, causing it to turn and run away. Miya coughed at the sharp smell of cayenne pepper. She scrambled backward, rubbing her eyes and wiping her nose on her sleeve.

Dropping the can of bear spray, Miya knelt beside Zoey.

"Are you okay, Zoey?"

Zoey raised her head and licked Miya's hand.

A tear slid down Miya's cheek. "You stay there. I'm going to grab the first aid kit." Miya pushed herself to her feet. She stood still for a second, waiting for her legs to stop shaking. As she turned toward Dream, Miya remembered—she had left the first aid kit in camp.

Miya groaned. "I don't have the first aid kit, Zoey, but I'll figure something out."

Miya ran to her saddlebag and pulled out the water bottle. She returned and threw herself down by Zoey. After fumbling for her pocketknife, Miya cut a strip off the bottom of her shirt. She soaked the fabric in water, parted Zoey's hair, and dabbed at the blood that saturated the fur on the collie's neck.

The damage wasn't as bad as Miya first thought. Dream's kick must have landed squarely on the coyote's head and neck. The coyote had punctured Zoey's skin, but her collar and thick hair had helped save her life. Miya wished for the antiseptic ointment and bandages in the first aid kit. She pressed her shirt firmly against the wound.

"I'm glad you're up to date on your shots. That coyote was acting so strange, I wonder if it had rabies." Miya stroked Zoey's forehead with her free hand. "What would I do if anything happened to you?"

Zoey whined and laid her head on her paws. After a few minutes, Miya cautiously lifted the square of cloth. The bleeding had nearly stopped. Miya ripped another strip of fabric and tied it around Zoey's neck. "I think you're ready to go. Do you want to ride with me?"

She gathered up Zoey and tried to boost her in front of the saddle, but Zoey squirmed out of Miya's arms. Miya set the collie back on the ground. "I know you don't like to ride. We'll walk slowly, and if you want, you can ride later."

After one more hug, Miya turned back to her horse and the trail ahead.

Still trembling, Miya climbed back on Dream. She winced as her knee hit the saddle. She pictured it—softball-sized, bruised, and puffy. Miya let her foot hang straight down. Eventually, she'd force herself to twist her knee and slip her boot into the stirrup.

In her mind's eye, Miya saw the first aid kit with the neon green vet wrap in its crinkly package. If she had a roll of it now, she'd bandage her knee so tightly that the throbbing would stop. Zoey would have a proper bandage, too, instead of Miya's shirt tail tied around her neck. Miya shook her head. She needed to let that bad decision go. She had bigger things to worry about.

Dream stuck her nose out, pulling the reins through Miya's fingers. "You're ready to go, huh?"

Miya breathed. A slow, deep breath in. A slow breath out.

Dream took a step toward the Summit. Miya grabbed her saddle string. She had chewed on it so much the end was frayed. Gathering her resolve, Miya loosened Dream's reins. "Tanner's waiting. Ready, Zoey?"

A few more miles to go, and they'd reach the top of Smith's Summit. Dream leaned into the mountain as she climbed. The wind gusted. Miya shoved her hat down harder on her forehead, then zipped her coat.

Snow began to fall again. Fumbling in her pocket for a granola bar, Miya tore it open with stiff fingers. The granola bar was dry and brittle from the cold. Miya spit it out and pocketed the rest.

As she rode along for hours without distraction, Miya had plenty of time to think. She considered her cache. When she'd started it, the first thing she'd put into her bottom desk drawer was the repaired sculpture of Dream. It represented the year she and the new girl, Abigail, had stood up to the bullies. *My anxiety is a kind of bully. It's trying to control me. Abigail and I beat the bullies once, so that proves I can overcome this new one, these fears, especially with Jake's help.*

With sudden fury, the wind tore through the trees, picking up snow and spinning it round and round in a circle. Sand and snow, pine needles, and twigs pelted Miya. She closed her eyes as the grit peppered her cheeks. *A different kind of grit helped me win my first barrel racing check.* After the other girls dismissed them because Miya and her horse were fat, she and Dream became bona fide contenders. Inwardly, she had the last laugh because the same kids who snickered when her family pulled up in an ancient stock trailer stopped giggling when Miya started winning.

Miya could almost smell the wildflowers Jake gave her on their second real date. She remembered the dimple playing across his cheek as he brought the bouquet from behind his back. The flowers were brittle now, pressed between the pages of her grandma's *Black Beauty* book, the third thing in her cache.

Jake. Aurora. Brinley. Miya's thoughts skipped in a new direction. *Why do those girls bother me so much? Yeah, they're loud and obnoxious, but lots of other kids are, too. They have cars, clothes, and money, so even the teachers let them get away with murder—everyone expects that with rich kids. So, what is it about Aurora and Brinley?*

She absently brushed the snow from her sleeve. *Maybe it's because Aurora and Brinley are in such a rush to claim Jake as one of their own, they trample over me. They don't see me as a person or even a worthy obstacle. That hurts. On the other hand, maybe I should listen to Jake when he tells me not to give the wrong people power over my life.*

Miya touched Dream's mane. "He's right," she said aloud. "From now on, Dream, I'll decide who influences my life."

She wasn't sure how to accomplish that, but stating the resolve out loud seemed like a good start.

The indentation of the trail in the snow was still visible. The animal tracks she'd been following were covered now. Except—Miya looked more closely—for one set. One fresh set of tracks. Black prints in the white snow. Palm-shaped. Five toes. Triangular claws.

Grizzly bear. The tracks were seven or eight inches across. A good-sized bear. Looking ahead, she saw a pile of bear scat steaming in the middle of the trail.

"Crap! Literally, crap!" *Is the bear just around the next switchback? Can I protect Zoey? How much bear spray is left?*

"Stop it, Miya," she said into the stillness. "It's just a big old boar, minding his own business and scarfing down food after the winter."

Yet Miya couldn't shake the feeling that unseen eyes watched her. She desperately wished for another can of bear spray.

No birds called. No squirrels chattered. The only sounds were the mare's footfalls, the squeak of her saddle, and the uneven rasp of Miya's breath.

"You okay back there, Zoey?" Miya called out. But the air, thick with snow, absorbed most of the sound. She closed her eyes to listen for the collie's response. Nothing.

"Zoey," Miya yelled again. She cocked her head, barely breathing. Zoey always answered. Always. Unless she couldn't.

The bear has Zoey! Zoey's hurt and weak. A giant grizzly has attacked her, and she's lying out there, bleeding in the snow!

Miya turned Dream around. "I'm coming, Zoey!" she screamed. Miya urged her mare to follow the tracks they'd made minutes ago. "Zoey!" Miya called. "Answer me, girl!"

Suddenly, the collie bounded out from behind the curtain of snow. She shook so hard that her tags rattled. She barked as though to say, "What do you need, boss?"

Relief sharpened Miya's tone. "Zoey, you stay right behind me now. There's a bear somewhere close."

Obediently, Zoey fell into line behind Dream.

Chapter Twenty-two

The higher they climbed, the more snow accumulated. Miya wondered if it had stormed all night and day. Dream plowed through drifts—some verging on three feet high. Steam rose from the mare's shoulders as the snow fell on them and melted.

Miya stopped Dream on a level spot. The game trail they'd been following had disappeared, buried under the snow.

Miya looked around. "Which way now, Dream?"

A raven cawed, brassy and loud. Then, the mountain grew silent. Miya ran her tongue around the inside of her mouth. She tasted the stale oatmeal of the granola bar. Miya reached up and scooped a handful of snow from a branch beside her. It trickled down her throat, tasting like pine and smelling of sap.

Miya shivered and hunched down into her saddle. She tasted the leather of her saddle string without knowing how it had gotten into her mouth. Dream lowered her muzzle as she and Zoey touched noses.

Dream took a few steps before angling to the right and sliding down a sidehill. "Since I don't have a plan, we'll go with your idea."

The mare continued, head down, taking cautious steps on the frozen ground. As they wound their way deeper into the woods, Miya ducked under the branches. Twice, she wasn't quick enough, so the pines slapped her cheek. The trail steepened, and Dream shortened her steps. Her nostrils flared in and out as the air thinned. When Dream stopped, Miya knew they were close to the summit.

The snowfall had lightened. A weak shaft of sunlight poked through a hole in the clouds. Miya took a deep breath, struggling to find her bearings. They were on a ridge above the timberline. Miya stared at the mountain to the north.

"Zoey! Look over there." Miya pointed. "That mountain looks just like Smith's Summit. But it can't be...can it?"

Miya's eyes scanned the peak to her left. Halfway up, she saw a ridge of red rock like the one on Smith's Summit. Below the ridge was the same bald spot, a treeless meadow. To the right was an unmistakably shaped rock—the one that looked like an elephant's head.

Miya swayed, her nerves jangling as if she'd drunk several cups of coffee. Dream pawed the ground, and Miya switched her gaze to the base of the mountain. From this angle, she saw the trail—a dark path heading upward from the trailhead and stopping at the camp on the opposite mountain.

"*No!*" Miya howled. "*No! No! No!*" She pounded on the saddle horn.

Miya knew it was easy to take a wrong turn, to follow a similar-looking game trail and end up on another ridge a mile or two or even five miles away from the planned destination. When that happened, a rider backtracked. Anyone who had spent time in the mountains had done the same thing. But how could that happen today? The day Tanner needed her, she'd wasted precious hours.

Retracing the route in her mind, Miya decided she had made the mistake back at the creek when she'd chosen the left fork of the trail instead of the right. No wonder she hadn't seen any land-marks. Now, it would be dark by the time Miya wound her way back to the spot. Then, she'd have to stop and build a fire while she waited for dawn. How would she manage that? Everything was soaked with snow.

Miya looked down into the draw that separated the ridges. As the crow flies, it was about a mile across—full of boulders, trees, and downed timber. Impassable. Miya had no choice but to retrace her steps for miles down the steep, slippery trail.

She slid off Dream and leaned into her warmth. A minute passed. Miya sank into the snow, burying her face in her hands.

"Come here, Zoey." Miya swallowed hard and laid her head against her collie's neck. "I'll get you some food, then we'll try to find our way back down." Miya checked Zoey's bandage. At least her dog wasn't bleeding anymore.

Miya closed her eyes and let the ways of exhaustion wash over her. Miya knew she had to return to the trail, and she would—soon.

Miya didn't know how much time had passed while she sat in the snow, the cold seeping into her bones. When her stomach growled, she pulled the partly eaten granola bar out and nibbled at it. She blew her nose on a damp tissue she'd dredged up from deep inside her coat pocket. Miya knew she needed to drink some water, feed Zoey, and get moving. Tanner was still counting on her. It was time to adjust the plan.

After pouring Zoey's dog food into a pile on the ground, Miya limped back to stuff the sandwich bag into her saddle bag. That was when she noticed a dark smudge in the snow. Her eyes traveled over the familiar shape, and despite her sore knee, she crouched down and laid her hand beside it.

A grizzly track. Miya pressed her hand into the snow. She compared the edges of her handprint with that of the edges of the grizzly track. Both were sharp instead of rounded. The bear was close.

Shivering, Miya pulled out the can of bear spray. She shook it, but it was impossible to tell how much was left. Miya knew the cans didn't hold much. Not enough to thwart an angry grizzly. Still, Miya reasoned, it might be better than nothing.

The air was heavy and damp. The breeze carried the scent of wet earth and the stronger skunk-like smell of the bear. Gripping the bear spray in her right hand, Miya followed the tracks that led into the draw between the two mountains.

"Good." Miya relaxed her hold on the can. "The bear's going in the opposite direction— he's headed down country."

A movement on the next ridge caught her eye. Four hundred yards away and ambling along with a pigeon-toed gait was the biggest grizzly Miya had ever seen. "He's beautiful," Miya said to Zoey. "I bet that bear weighs eight hundred pounds." She watched the grizzly enter the woods and emerge a minute later. Headed toward the Summit.

With an effort, Miya climbed on Dream. Her back ached, and her eyes were gritty. She closed them for an instant. When she opened her eyes, Miya realized she was staring at Smith's Summit—and something else.

Sitting tall in the saddle, Miya squinted and shook her head. There was no mistake. From this angle, she could see a black stripe of trail leading the mountain and across a windswept meadow. It appeared to join the original trail at the top.

Miya stared at the path so hard her gaze blurred. *Is this the horse trail the old timers talked about, or am I imagining a path over the Summit because I want it so badly?* Miya closed her eyes, counted to ten, took five slow breaths, and opened them. Yes! The path was still there.

"But Dream, that trail isn't doing us a bit of good because we have to cross this draw to get to it, and we can't." Miya stared down at the bear tracks. "Or can we?"

Miya knew riders and hikers often met bears on the trail because bears, like people, usually take the easiest route. She also knew the grizzly was probably angling down country to hit a path on the other side.

Should I take a huge chance and follow these tracks? Who knows what I might find at the bottom of the draw? And what if I lose the tracks? I'll be lost in the tangle of trees and boulders with nighttime coming on.

Reaching into her vest pocket, Miya touched the bag of grizzly fur. *If we just make it across the draw, I can call for help within the next several hours instead of waiting another night and day.*

In her mind, Miya heard her father's incredulous voice. "Are you seriously going to chase after a grizzly bear?"

"Think of it as following Ursa Minor, Dad."

She tapped Dream with her heels. The mare didn't hesitate. She took a step, following the bear's tracks. Dream took a second step and a third. Her course didn't waver even when the tracks doubled back around a boulder and out of sight. Because of the danger, Miya concentrated so hard on the tracks she barely heard the warning.

"Huff. Huff."

Miya froze. What was that? A clicking sound and a woof. *Sounds like a bear*, Miya thought, *but the grizzly is way ahead of me…unless there's another one… or a wolf or a coyote.*

Zoey growled. Miya's breath quickened. Dream backed up. One step. Two. Miya pulled out the can of bear spray. Motionless, she stared into the shadows.

Miya spoke to Zoey in a whisper. "If anything happens to me, do not chase that animal. Go back to Jake for help."

Zoey whined. Miya hoped her dog understood. Several minutes passed. The woods were silent, watchful, waiting.

The undergrowth rustled as the animal moved. Heart pounding, Miya waited. Would it charge toward her or head down another trail?

Another few minutes passed while Miya held her breath. Thankfully, nothing appeared.

She dismounted and studied the new set of tracks. "I think those belong to a black bear. The tracks are much smaller, and there's more space between the toes and the foot, but I could be wrong, Zoey."

"Let's try it again, Dream." She mounted the horse and followed the tracks heading toward the Summit. "Don't crowd the bear in front of us. We've been warned."

The hairs on Miya's arms rose as Dream moved forward. She knew black bears weren't as aggressive as grizzlies, but she still searched the trees in case the bear doubled back.

Miya closed her eyes, listening hard. The snow amplified the harsh sound of her breath and the swish of the bear as it moved through the underbrush. When the bear's rustling stopped, Miya stopped. Each time, she waited for him to move off again. When he did, she followed.

The breeze stirred, carrying with it a definite bear smell. Wrinkling her nose, Miya waited until he finally turned south, away from the Summit.

Chapter Twenty-three

Half an hour later, Miya rode out of the timber. She gazed at the side of the mountain. One more hill to climb. A steep one, but once they topped it, she, Dream, and Zoey would be at the top of the Summit.

Miya eyed the five hundred feet of slippery trail. It was a narrow path, nearly straight up, used by mountain sheep instead of horses. Miya was tempted to step off Dream and climb, to feel the earth under her feet. But if she started sliding, she trusted Dream's balance more than her own.

The trail was steeper than the one she'd taken weeks ago in pursuit of the elk antler and much more vertical than Wildcat Pass. Jake wasn't here to lead her over it today. She had to ride with her eyes wide open.

It was hot. Miya tugged at her neck scarf. As the world started to spin, she glimpsed flashes of blue sky mixed with rock, snow, and wind-swept junipers. She closed her eyes and gripped her saddle horn. *You will not have a panic attack. You will not throw up.* Miya breathed in deeply for a count of five seconds, held her breath for five, and breathed out slowly. *You're not the same person you were two days ago, so stop worrying and start moving.* Miya breathed deeply again.

"Dream, I trust you one hundred percent, but whatever you do, don't look over the edge and don't stop." Miya leaned forward and loosened her reins. She concentrated on the bear's footprints in front of her. Dream stepped across the first track. "I am smart, I am strong, and I am going to make it to the top of this mountain," Miya spoke as Dream climbed.

The blood pounded in her ears. "We've gone fifty feet," Miya whispered. Her voice shook, but the words still gave her courage. She'd concentrate on Tanner instead of the shifting rock beneath her. "I didn't freak out when Tanner had his asthma attack." Miya's mouth was dry, but she kept talking to her horse and dog. "Jake has faith in me. He said I could do this, and I can."

Dream stumbled over rocks—brown, gray, and rust-colored. Some rocks were as fine as sand, others the size of a large, clenched fist, and still others the size of dinner plates. Miya's stomach lurched when Dream tripped. Somehow, Dream regained her footing and kept moving forward.

"One more curve." Her legs trembled as much as her voice. "A short straight away, and it's downhill to the trailhead."

Miya released the breath she'd been holding. After she rounded the bend, Dream stopped, ears forward, snorting. Taken by surprise, Miya rocked against the front of the saddle. A large granite ledge lay across the trail above. It was shaped like a giant stair step, at least two feet higher than the path. The outcropping was gray and white, striped with black. Miya rode closer. The initial jump onto the ledge was about two feet, but the slick surface of the rock continued for twenty more feet, straight up the mountain.

The bear had scrambled over it, but it would be almost impossible for a horse carrying a girl. Miya looked behind her. The trail was so narrow she doubted she could turn around.

While Dream struggled to keep her balance on the side of the slope, Miya heard her dad's voice as clearly as though he were riding beside her. "Get off that horse right now. She's going to fall. Slide down to the next switchback on your butt, and let Dream and Zoey find their own way."

"But Dad," Miya argued. "Is the mountain truly impassable, or does it just look that way because I'm so scared?"

"You should be scared, Miya. A horse can't dig into solid rock, only skate along the top. One misstep and you'll kill yourself and Dream."

"This is the scariest thing I've ever done, Dream, but if I ride back to camp without getting help, Tanner could be the one to die. We've got this, Dream. Climb as though our lives depend upon it."

Her heart thumped painfully against her ribs as she shifted her weight forward in the saddle. Dream didn't hesitate. She lunged at the ledge. Metal shoes scraped the stone surface. Sparks, yellow and blue, flew from Dream's shoes as she struggled to gain purchase on the slick rock. It smelled of sulfur as though a match had been struck.

Dream fell back, unable to scale the outcropping. For an instant, she teetered on her hind legs until Miya realized the paint was falling over backward. Miya jerked her foot out of the left stirrup and struggled to push herself away. She glimpsed a collage of Dream's ears, muddy earth, darkening sky. Miya heard a whimpering sound and realized it was coming from her.

With an enormous effort, Dream bunched her muscles and flung herself at the ledge again. Caught by surprise, Miya almost fell out of the saddle. She recovered quickly, found her stirrup, and focused all her energy on the rock and sky above. "Go, Dream, go!"

One of Dream's ears swiveled back, the other pointed forward. With a surge, the paint jumped onto the top of the ledge. Without pausing, Dream threw herself at the side of the mountain. The rocks rolled and bounced off the trail. Dream pushed forward, her saddle squeaking as she strained against her breast collar. Inch by inch, Dream clawed her way up twenty steep feet. Clinging to her mane, Miya whispered a mixture of prayers and encouragement.

When they reached the top of the ridge, Dream's sides heaved as her nostrils flared in and out. Miya slid to the ground and hugged the paint. Heart. Courage. Trust. Her horse had more of those three qualities than most people had. "You saved us, Dream. Maybe you saved Tanner, too."

Miya was cold, but a feeling of warmth pumped through her veins. "Those words belong to us now. Heart. Courage. Trust."

Miya turned her face toward the sky. The setting sun touched her cheeks as she looked at the last few miles leading to the trailhead—a wide trail with gentle switchbacks.

Dream's ears pricked up. She swung her head around. Zoey barked. One ridge over, Miya saw a round black shape swaying back and forth as he made his way down the trail in front of her.

"Hey," Miya cupped her hands around her mouth and yelled. "Hey, bear!" Her voice carried across the mountain stillness. The grizzly stopped and stood on his hind legs, peering back over his shoulder at her. "Thanks for guiding us home!"

The bear waited a heartbeat, dropped to all fours, and disappeared.

Chapter Twenty-four

It was dark by the time Miya and Dream arrived at the trailhead. She unsaddled her horse and loaded her into the trailer. Zoey jumped into the passenger seat of Jake's truck. Miya found the spare key and fitted it into the ignition.

Like all farm kids, Miya had driven ranch vehicles from the time she could perch on the edge of her seat and touch the pedals with her tiptoes. She knew navigating a twisty, narrow road, traveling downhill while hauling a horse trailer wasn't going to be easy.

Still, she needed to find cell reception and find it quickly. Miya eased off the emergency brake, pulled to the front of the trailhead, and looked both ways. The headlights bounced along the guardrail across from her. Along its length were dents, where vehicles had misjudged the steep turns or slid out of control in the ice and snow.

"I can do this if I keep my eyes on the road. No looking over the side. Slow and steady."

Miya swiped her sweaty palms down her thighs. She clutched the wheel with both hands. Steering around the first hairpin turn, Miya peered into the inky darkness. The dim glow of the headlights barely cut through the darkness. Miya scooted forward in her seat, squinting through the windshield. She didn't want to hit a deer, an elk, or, heaven forbid, a bear. Rolling her head from side to side, she thought, *Ten more miles. I can pull off and make a call.*

After crawling around the next curve, Miya downshifted. The grade ahead was steep, and a two-thousand-pound horse trailer pushed her from behind. "Zoey, what if my brakes heat up and I lose them? I'll drive off the side of the mountain."

"Stop with the what-ifs." Miya berated herself. She breathed deeply and said, "Heart. Courage. Trust." Miya swallowed. "Besides, there are runaway truck ramps along here, so if worst comes to worst I'll bury this rig up to its axles in sand." She thought about the truck ramps for a few seconds before abandoning that idea. She couldn't call a tow truck to extricate the rig until the next morning. It would take forever to walk ten miles for help. During that time, Tanner might have another attack.

Miya crept around the next switchback. "We should be nearly there, Zoey."

Up ahead, Miya glimpsed the outline of a ponderosa pine perched precariously on a rock shelf. "Lone tree?" she asked in disbelief. "Lone Tree? Why aren't we miles past that by now? Yes, I'm going slow, and it's hard to see, but I was sure we'd made it farther than Lone Tree!"

Miya pressed the accelerator so the truck lurched forward. "Whoa!" Miya said, immediately withdrawing her boot from the pedal. "Bad idea. I'm going to have to accept the fact that it's going to take longer than I thought to drive down this mountain. A lot longer." Breathe. Stay calm. Patience will win in the end.

When she finally heard the cacophony of notifications chiming on her phone, Miya laughed. She would have high-fived Zoey but needed to keep both hands on the wheel. Miya slowed down so she wouldn't miss the next pull-off. When she was finally parked, Miya stared at the phone. She wanted to hear her mom and dad's voices, but now was not the time. She had to try Janelle's number first. She had to know if Janelle had made it out of the mountains.

Miya's hand shook. "Please let her be okay," Miya whispered. "Please."

Mya's knee bumped up and down as she waited long seconds to be connected.

"Is that you? Miya, is that really you?" The relief in Janelle's voice filled the truck.

"Yes! It's me! I'm sitting at the pull-off by mile marker seventeen. Before I tell you the whole story, though, call a helicopter to rescue Tanner."

"Give me the rescue details. I'll contact the hospital. I'll call you back after that. Five minutes."

While Janelle notified the air ambulance, Miya phoned her mom and dad. "I made it out of the mountains. I'm at mile marker seventeen."

"We're on our way," her dad said before Miya could say anything more.

Mom's warm voice came over the phone. "We'll be there soon. We're about to lose reception, so stay put. We love you."

While she waited for her mom and dad, Miya called Janelle back. The first thing she did was assure her that Jake was unhurt. Then, Miya asked about Janelle's ride back to camp.

Janelle explained. "I reached the edge of the slide at about 1:00 in the morning. Between the sliver of the moon and my flashlight, I could see there was no way I could make it across, so I turned around. I reached the trailhead at daylight. I was on the phone with the Forest Service when they opened. They've had a crew out there ever since."

"Jake's going to be so relieved that you're okay." Miya laid her head against the window. "By the way, how's Comet?"

"Like you, she's just fine."

Something cold and wet poked her cheek. Through a haze of sleep, Miya reached up to push it away. Whiskers and warm breath tickled her face. Breath that smelled of dog food. Miya opened one eye.

"Zoey," she groaned. "Go away. I'm tired."

Miya's eyes moved to the heap of dirty clothes on the floor. Suddenly, she remembered. Tanner! Throwing aside her covers, Miya fell out of bed and stumbled to the door. Had Tanner been rescued? She tried to stay awake and wait for the news last night, but her eyes kept slamming shut.

At the top of the staircase, Miya gripped the railing and without hesitation limped down the stairs as fast as her swollen knee allowed. Bursting into the kitchen, Miya found her dad sitting at the table and talking on his phone.

"Glad to hear it. Keep us updated. Bye."

Miya sank into a chair. "Glad to hear what?"

Smiling, Dad stood up and dropped a kiss on top of her head. "Good morning to you, too."

"Good morning, Dad. Glad to hear what?"

"Tanner's going to be fine. Although the ER doctor told Parker that between not having inhalers and the altitude and cold air, he wasn't sure Tanner would have survived much longer up there."

Dropping her head onto her folded arms, Miya whispered, "That's scary."

After a short pause, Miya felt Dad's hand on her shoulder. "You did good, Miya. I'm proud of you."

Miya lifted her head and put her hand over his. "Thanks, Dad, but I made some mistakes, and I want to tell you about them. For one thing, I left the Inreach behind, I didn't shut the drift fence, and..."

"You can tell me all that later," her dad interrupted. "The bottom line is Tanner's alive because of you." Dad moved to the stove and opened the oven. "Your mom made breakfast for you before she left for work. Hungry?"

"Starving! How are things going with clearing the trail?"

Her dad set a plate heaped with pancakes, eggs, and bacon in front of her before replying. "They hope to have it passable by late tomorrow or early the next day. Jake stayed behind to take care of the horses. As soon as it's clear, we'll ride in and help pack out camp."

Jake. Miya smiled. Now that he knows his mother is okay, he'll be perfectly content up there. She pictured him humming as he brushed the horses. Behind him, cotton candy clouds drifted in and out of the valleys and over the ridge of Smith's Summit.

"Dad, I couldn't have done it without Jake."

Her dad nodded. "I know. Accepting other people's help is part of growing up."

He sipped his coffee. "By the way, this bit of news will blow your mind. Parker seems to be good friends with the CEO of Adventure Today, one of those outdoor destination travel companies. Their VP called to discuss contracting with us. They want to hire Skippingbird Outfitters to take bimonthly fishing trips."

Miya put down her fork. "You're kidding. Do they pay well?"

He nodded. "They do. I need to look into it more, but if I accept their offer, I'll be hiring a new fishing guide. Do you think you might be interested?"

Miya grinned as she buttered her pancake. "To quote Jake, 'I think I could be persuaded.'"

Epilogue

Two weeks later, Miya sighted down a two by four outside Kemplers' garage. She had called the courthouse and discovered their rental was just outside the city limits, where it was legal to raise poultry. She'd gathered a crew of volunteers to help build a duck coop roomy enough for Baby Shark's friends to join him later this summer. Adelita's mom suggested they paint the coop bright purple, Adelita's favorite color.

"No, we can't use this one. It's warped." Miya handed the board to Jake and picked up another off the stack.

Jake shrugged and added it to a growing pile of rejects. "Miya, we're not building a palace."

"Yes, we are." Tanner adjusted the kid's size tool belt around his waist. "It's going to be a Taj Mahal for Baby Shark. Adelita will be so surprised when she gets back from her grandma's."

Miya smiled at him. After being airlifted off the mountain, Tanner remained hospitalized for three days. Compared to her sturdy cousins, Tanner still seemed fragile to her. She cocked her head and listened to him breathe. *At least he's not wheezing, but we'll keep him in the fresh air, out of the sawdust.* "Why don't you sit on that bucket for a minute?"

Tanner nodded and plopped down on the overturned bucket. Now that he was spending more time with his dad, he seemed happier. He'd added several items to his cache and was excited about the after-school chess club and about joining the robotics team.

Mr. Parker sanded a board laid across two sawhorses. "I think this is smooth enough."

Miya ran her fingertips over the wood. "Almost." She folded a piece of sandpaper in quarters and handed it to him. "You can go over it with a finer grit."

Mr. Parker rolled his eyes. "I'll do it in a minute, Miss Perfection, although I'm sure Baby Shark will be fine with the board the way it is." He reached into his pocket and withdrew his phone. "I need to make a quick call first."

"Dad!" Tanner jumped off the bucket. "Remember you promised this was a phone-free zone."

"Oops! Sorry. Forgot. Old habits die hard." He slipped the phone back into his pocket. "Do you want to help me sand this board?"

Tanner selected a piece of sandpaper and folded it. "Yep. Anything for Baby Shark's new castle."

"How about this one, Miss Perfection?" Jake teased as he held up another board.

Miya elbowed him lightly in the side. "It looks fine. I'll mark it." Miya slid the pencil from behind her ear and held it between her thumb and forefinger, remembering the sketch she'd drawn in her journal last night.

The picture was of her and Jake, holding hands and riding their horses toward the mountain. Zoey trotted alongside them. There were no monsters in the picture. Miya knew she'd have to confront her anxiety, but she was grateful she had some tools to help her now.

A shiny silver Toyota Tundra pulled up as Miya and Jake measured another two by four.

"Hey, Jake, why haven't you texted me back?" Brinley strolled up to Jake and pouted. "We all wanted to hear about the big rescue."

His brown eyes dancing with mischief, Jake pulled off his gloves and leaned toward Brinley. "The B.I.G. rescue. Brace yourself, and I'll give you a recap of everything I did." Pausing for effect, Jake deadpanned. "I stayed in camp. Wasn't that epic of me?" He pointed to Tanner. "Miya was the one who rode out and saved this kid's life. By herself."

By herself. The words echoed in Miya's head. She smiled. She knew she hadn't been by herself. She'd had Dream, Zoey, and the help of a rather large grizzly bear. She opened her mouth and closed it before correcting Jake. She doubted Brinley would understand.

Miya glanced at the three girls, carbon copies of Aurora and Brinley, crammed into the pickup, scrolling through their phones. At that moment, Miya truly understood she didn't need the wealth or approval of those girls. She was grateful for Jake, a few good friends, her horse, and her dog. She didn't need those kids on social media, and she didn't need them in person.

She was Miya Skippingbird with a place in her community, both human and wild. A place of hope, challenge, and possibility. She had her cache to prove it.

"What was the name of that mountain again?" Brinley asked Jake.

"Most people call it Smith's Summit," Jake took Miya's hand, "but we call it Miya's Mountain."

Study Questions

1. In Chapter One, Miya's mother accuses her of not taking responsibility. Do you think this is valid? Why or why not?

2. In Chapter Two, Miya is petrified of sliding off the side of the mountain. Think of a time when you were frightened. Describe the situation and how you responded.

3. When Miya's father picks her up, he is deeply disappointed and reacts strongly. Do you think his reaction is fair? Why or why not?

4. Why do you think Miya doesn't eat the Snickers bar her father brought her?

5. Find examples in Chapter Five which demonstrate the beginning of Miya's fear of heights.

Chapters 4-5

1. Jake and Janelle Runningdeer are introduced in Chapter Five. How would you describe these two characters?

2. How does Miya feel after she isn't able to video Jake's ride? How does Jake react?

3. Have you ever been to a rodeo? What are some of the sights and sounds you saw and heard?

4. Research Sugar Gliders. Do you think you'd like one for a pet? Why or why not?

5. Who are Aurora and Brinley, and how does Miya feel about them? How do you think Jake feels about them?

Chapters 6-8

1. Who are Adalita and Jennifer Kempler? Who is Baby Shark? Why does Miya offer to take Baby Shark home?

2. At this point in the novel, what steps is Miya taking to overcome her fear?

3. Why do you think Miya's barrel run turns out so poorly?

4. Miya's father finally consents to her leading the pack trip. Why do you think he agrees? If you were her father, would you agree?

5. Describe Mr. Parker and Tanner. What can you infer about their personalities at this point in the novel?

Chapters 9-10

1. Why won't Miya accept Jake's help in preparing for the trip?

2. Why does Miya sketch in a journal?

3. Think of an event that you are or were concerned about. Draw a quick sketch of the event. Does drawing the picture make you feel differently about the event?

4. How does Miya feel about Janelle leaving to take Comet to the vet?

5. How does Mr. Parker act at the trailhead? Support your answer by finding examples in the text.

Chapters 11-12

1. Why is it concerning that Mr. Parker dropped the Explorer in the river?

2. Choose one student to be Miya, and another to be Jake. Each student will try to convince the other of the wisdom to either wait the full thirty minutes before venturing across Wildcat Pass or riding across after fifteen minutes.

3. What are some of the strategies Miya used to help overcome her anxiety and ride across Wildcat Pass?

Chapters 13-15

1. Retell Mr. Parker's childhood camping adventure.

2. Have you ever gone camping? If so, what was the best/worst part?

3. What does Miya learn about Tanner's health and about his relationship with his father?

4. Why is the normally unflappable Jake so upset at the end of Chapter 15?

Chapters 16-17

1. Each character has concerns about being trapped by the rockslide. Name the worries each person is harboring. What would be most concerning to you if you were in that situation?

2. What is a cache, and why is it significant to Miya and Tanner?

3. If you had a cache, list the items that you would include.

Chapters 18-20

1. What changes Miya's mind about attempting to ride out over Smith's Summit?

2. Does Jake support Miya's decision? Why or why not?

3. Do you think it is wise for Miya to attempt the ride out over Smith's Summit? Why or why not?

4. Describe a time when you were lost or thought you were lost. Compare your feelings to Miya's as she searches for the chimney-shaped rocks.

Chapters 21-Epilogue

1. What decision does Miya make about Aurora and Brinley?

2. When Miya looks across the mountain in Chapter 22, what does she discover? How does she feel?

3. Miya decides to follow the bear in Chapter 51. Do you think this was a wise choice? Why or why not?

4. Make a timeline of the bears' interaction with the pack trip. Why do you think the author included the bears?

5. What do you think Miya means when she says that she's found her place in the community, both human and wild?

6. In the Epilogue, Miya says that she knows she'll have to confront anxiety again, but now she has some tools to help her. Name three things that helped her handle her anxiety.

Acknowledgments

I'd like to express my sincere appreciation to the following people for all of their support:

The Tillery family, Becca, Brandon, Stetson, and Denali. The Whisler family, Alex, Ashley, Ryder, Ridge, and River. Thank you for always being in my corner.

I'd like to thank Jennifer Just for reading and commenting on the first drafts. I'd also like to thank Kathy Bjornestad, Ann Sanders, Anna Poe, Marsha Neubert, and especially Bonnie Craig for reviewing subsequent drafts.

I truly appreciate the members of my writing group at the Cody Public Library. Month after month, facilitated by our fearless leader, Emma Blottenberger, these aspiring authors provided invaluable feedback.

I own a debt of gratitude to the Shoshone Back Country Horsemen who tirelessly work alongside the Forest Service keeping the trails accessible for folks to experience the back country.

Although I've never met her in person, I'd like to thank my Facebook friend Denise Alverez. Her podcast, "How to Market Your Horse Business," has inspired me with goal setting, content, and social media ideas. I also admire her tireless efforts to start a facility for at-risk teens with horses.

I'd like to thank my editor, Patricia Phillips.

Most of all, thank you to Von Ringler for his unwavering support and suggestions. Everyone needs a "Jake" in their life, and he's always been mine.

About the Author

Cathy Ringler is a storyteller, cowgirl, and former teacher. She lives at the foot of the beautiful Beartooth Mountains and rides in them as often as her busy schedule will allow. *Miya's Mountain* is the gripping sequel of *Miya's Dream*. Miya continues to grapple with bullying, but now she must face crippling anxiety.

An award-winning author, Cathy's first book, *Miya's Dream*, received a bronze medal in the Moonbeam Awards, third place in the Colorado Evvy awards, and a BlueInk Starred Review. *Miya's Dream* was also featured in a Wyoming PBS segment on bullying.

Cathy enjoys working with youth. She's presented writing workshops at several schools as well as local libraries. She enjoys the role of Education Director for the Shoshone Backcountry Horsemen. This position allows her to promote the principles of Leave No Trace, safety, and conservation of the back country. She also tells stories of adventures on horseback at the annual Wyoming Discovery Days Festival.

In the summertime, Cathy can be found riding her horse along wilderness trails, camping in the meadows, and jotting down stories by lantern light.

Visit her at **cathyringler.com**.

www.ingramcontent.com/pod-product-compliance
Lightning Source LLC
Chambersburg PA
CBHW030255270626
47156CB00022B/2764